MW00767973

FEATURING STORIES BY

ANGIE HODAPP · BETSY DORNBUSCH · CARRIE VAUGHN
MARIO ACEVEDO · SAM W. ANDERSON · SEAN EADS
STEPHEN GRAHAM JONES · TRAVIS HEERMANN
WARREN HAMMOND

AFTERWORD BY BRIAN KEENE

EDITED BY JEANNE C. STEIN AND JOSHUA VIOLA

HEX PUBLISHERS

This is a work of fiction. All characters, organizations, and events portrayed in this book are products of the authors' imaginations and/or are used fictitiously.

GEORGETOWN HAUNTS AND MYSTERIES

Copyright © 2017 by Hex Publishers, LLC.

All rights reserved.

"Harry and Marlowe Versus the Haunted Locomotive of the Rockies" copyright © 2014 by Carrie Vaughn. All other stories are original to this volume and are copyright © 2017 to their respective authors.

Edited by Jeanne C. Stein and Joshua Viola

Copyedits by Jennifer Melzer
Cover design by Kirk DouPonce
Typesets and formatting by Dustin Carpenter

A Hex Publishers Book

Published & Distributed by Hex Publishers, LLC

PO BOX 298
Erie, CO 80516

www.HexPublishers.com

No portion of this book may be reproduced without first obtaining the permission of the copyright holder.

Print ISBN-10: 0-9986667-5-0
Print ISBN-13: 978-0-9986667-5-4
Ebook ISBN-10: 0-9986667-6-9
Ebook ISBN-13: 978-0-9986667-6-1

First Edition: June 2017

10 9 8 7 6 5 4 3 2 1

Printed in the U.S.A.

IN MEMORY OF TOM PICCIRILLI

ACKNOWLEDGMENTS

Thanks to Mike Hance, Jhonette Perdue, J.L. Benet, and all of the fine folks at the Ghost Town Writers Retreat for inspiring this anthology.

CONTENTS

Introduction by Jeanne C. Stein and Joshua Viola   7

Deep Veins by Travis Heermann   9

The Silver Belle by Betsy Dornbusch   29

A Bouquet of Wonder and Marvel by Sean Eads   53

Price Brothers Fine Portraiture: 78
Still Life by Warren Hammond

Price Brothers Fine Portraiture: 88
Afterlife by Angie Hodapp

Harry and Marlowe Versus the Haunted   101
Locomotive of the Rockies by Carrie Vaughn

Argentine Pass by Stephen Graham Jones   137

The Madam in Room 217 by Sam W. Anderson   153

Her First Husband by Mario Acevedo   171

Afterword by Brian Keene   183

About The Editors   190

INTRODUCTION

JEANNE C. STEIN & JOSHUA VIOLA

The mountain peaks are steep, the mines are deep, and between them evil creeps—

A lot of us grew up in the shadows of these mountains. We tend to see them as a mythic space, the mountain peaks protecting us from not only the prevailing winds that bring storms and snow to the flatlands, but also from a mass culture that threatens the rugged sense of individuality found in many a small mountain town.

Georgetown, for instance.

And what small mountain town would be complete without its share of hauntings?

Georgetown's history is chock-a-block with unexplained occurrences, but we decided to add more. We asked a distinguished panel of authors to contribute to the town's myth and mystery by coming up with their own haunts. The results were beyond our expectations.

So soak up the atmosphere of the stories inside this anthology—inspired by the first-ever Georgetown Ghost Town Writers Retreat—and settle back with a cup of coffee or a crystal glass of whiskey and enjoy the wild musings of the authors' imaginations. But don't look over your shoulder. You never know who might be lurking there.

DEEP VEINS

TRAVIS HEERMANN

1861
COLORADO TERRITORY

The candlelight flickered as Frank hammered the drill into the milky vein of quartz. Emmet held the drill granite-steady on his right shoulder, twisting the drill a quarter turn after each of Frank's blows. Frank's gaze fastened upon the mushroomed steel butt of the drill as he swung the sixteen-pound sledge, driving the drill point deeper, deeper, until it would reach sufficient depth to fill the cavity with black powder and blast away.

Emmet's face was a mask of concentration while holding the drill for the hammer blows, a stolid dispassion born of the kind of trust that only a brother could carry. A missed swing could cause severe injury for both of them. The cramped shaft did not allow enough freedom of movement to hold oneself well clear.

Then a blow drove the drill deep, out of Emmet's hands.

"We punched through," Emmet said.

"Looks like," Frank said.

Emmet worked his leather-gloved fingers around the drill shaft and tried to prize it out of the hole, allowing Frank a moment's respite to set down the hammer. His shoulders and back were a mass of aching knots, as always by this time of day. He tipped back his canvas hat, careful not to disturb the flame of the small oil lamp resting upon the leather brim, and wiped the sweat from his brow. The heat of the lamp warmed his head uncomfortably, but no one partial to a life of soft splendor decided to scratch the Yellow out of the earth.

Emmet yanked the drill out of the hole, and a blast of tainted air followed, a strange fetid stench. He clamped a glove over his face. The invisible miasma swirled around Frank, the power of it punching him in the nostrils, getting thicker rather than abating, until his breast seized tight. Emmet hooked an arm under Frank's and pulled him away.

"Let's go! Come on!" Emmet cried. Frank finally got his feet under him, and they ran together.

Emanations of deadly gases from the bowels of the earth were a well-known hazard to hard-rock miners, and the Grubbs boys didn't have a canary to serve as a warning. The tunnel stretched toward the waning daylight. Their feet splashed in the constant trickles of water on the floor.

For the full two hundred feet to the surface, first a hundred a feet of dense, solid granite, and then the last hundred feet of slide, as the loose surface boulders and earth was called, the stench hounded them like the putrescence of a hundred open graves, but mixed with some earthy, metallic tang. They ran hunched over to make sure they didn't bash their heads into a low-hanging knob of granite or ceiling beam.

They burst into their camp, gagging and coughing. Fading light the color of the metal they sought filtered over the forested peaks of the valley. A warm breeze swept away the lingering stench, fluttering the roof of their tent, and whispering through the leaves of a nearby aspen grove. The mountainside lay as quiet as Eden. Far below their claim lay the silver thread of Clear Creek, meandering through boulders and forest. Fifty yards to the left lay the burbling stream they used to sluice the gold flake from pulverized quartz. Twenty yards to the right, Sniffles the burro watched them placidly from his long tether.

"You all right, Frank?" Emmet coughed.

Frank nodded.

Emmet was the younger of the two brothers, but shorter and sturdier, built like a buffalo rather than a gawky mule deer. Frank even had the ears to match, sticking out of his head like a stagecoach with the doors open.

Frank said, "We'll give it a mite to let it air out." He took a deep breath to help clear the ache out of his lungs.

Meanwhile Emmet poured some of this morning's coffee into a mug, swished it around, and swallowed. "I can still taste it."

Frank reached for the cup and Emmet handed it over.

The coffee was cold and bitter, like Frank's soul would be if they didn't manage to find more than dregs soon. After five months of digging, they'd found only enough gold to whet their appetites, only enough to pay for the most basic supplies. They hadn't hit anything big. A couple of outfits had landed good results from placer mines down in the valley, but the Grubb brothers had staked their claim far enough from the Georgetown camp to discourage claim jumpers.

Emmet must have seen the thoughts on Frank's face. "Don't worry. We'll hit soon. The color was too good to leave us disappointed for long."

"Unless that assayer was a crook," Frank said. He hadn't liked the gaunt look in that man's eye.

"Why would he lie to us?"

"Take our money. Keep us guessing until the bigger fish swallow us whole."

A promising chunk of quartz back in March had netted them fifty dollars in gold flake and prompted them to pour their full energy into this spot, this claim, this pinhole in the earth. But the gold had dried up. All these weeks of back-breaking work, feeling like they were looking for water in the desert, had taken a toll on his spirit.

"You reckon she'll wait for me?" Frank said.

"Good Christ, Frank," Emmet said with an exasperated sigh.

Frank knew it was a well-worn topic of conversation but he needed some hope to cling to.

Emmet said, "We're going back to Georgetown so filthy rich she'll smell us coming all the way from the Clear Creek fork. Maybe that void we just hit will open up into the mother lode."

"You think so?"

"I know it. I feel it in my bones."

Frank nodded, the reassurances assuaging the ache of overtaxed muscles and over-yearning heart. Mollie Hogan's smile sparkled in his memory like a vein of pure silver, a forest of red hair and speckling of freckles across a dainty nose like the red earth of the Kansas Territory, or Colorado Territory, or whatever they were calling it nowadays. His plug-ugly countenance had never brought the young ladies beating a path to his door. Until Mollie gave him the kind of smile that opened doors in him and lured him out to speak to her, and she found him agreeable enough to spend an afternoon picnicking at Mount Prospect Hill Cemetery. Her hand was calloused and strong when he took it and told her he was going to marry her, that he was going to make her a rich woman. She had laughed, a fine musical sound without disdain in it, and told him it was a pleasant sentiment. She would come with him to Georgetown. Doubtless there was a living to be made as a laundress and cook among the unwashed miners. But she couldn't marry every man who made a similar claim in a time when gold fever was drawing hundreds, thousands of men from the east. A woman with a pleasing face and healthy figure heard more than her share of such declarations of love. "I'll wait for you in Georgetown. You come back with something, Frank Grubbs. I believe in you."

The longing to kiss her that day now paled in comparison to his regret that hadn't had the guts to do it, nor on the ride into the mountains. How many times had he dreamed of stealing a kiss?

"Let's go blast that hole and see what's on the other side," Emmet said, drawing Frank out of his habitual train of thoughts.

❦

The blast opened a two-foot hole into a black nothingness.

Frank peered into the hole while Emmet went to retrieve lanterns from their tent. The light from his oil lamp on his hat met nothing but blackness. The thickness of the wall, about two feet, prevented peering deeply into the beyond. It would take some clearing away. The hour was growing late and his muscles taxed, but he took up his pick axe and set about expanding the opening. The quartz gave way to his steel, and when Emmet returned they made quick progress, until one of them could slip through the hole.

An uncommon excitement kicked Frank's heart into a higher speed as he slid headfirst through the opening, lantern extended on one arm, the rock digging into ribs and forearms as he wormed forward. The brighter light of the lantern revealed a cavern of extensive dimensions, and their opening was situated about fifteen feet above the floor. Pale, stone fangs from ceiling and floor caught the yellow-orange glow. The air was moist, and dripping water echoed through the space.

Frank withdrew and said, "We need the rope. I'm going in to take a quick gander."

"Are you sure? It's getting late and we're both tired."

"We surely ain't found any gold today. This is too curious to go to sleep on."

Emmet went back for rope, and they secured it to a hook driven into a fissure. He wanted to follow Frank inside, but Frank stopped him. "One of us needs to stay here and haul me up. The hole is too high to reach from below. If our hook works loose, we're dead men."

Emmet's head bobbed in acknowledgment, so Frank went feet-first through the hole this time, and Emmet lowered him down.

When his feet touched the floor and he backed away from the wall, he surveyed the chamber. The walls sparkled with crystalline stars reflecting his lantern light, or the eyes of a thousand night creatures watching him from the shadows.

Above, Emmet whistled with awe. "Sure is pretty."

The stench from before forced Frank to breathe through his shirt, unpleasant but bearable.

The cavern narrowed and squeezed down some hundred feet from the hole, forcing him to bend at the waist, rough stone scraping across his back. One of the walls gleamed like pristine quartz, shades of milky white and pink, darkening to streaks of amethyst. He was no expert on precious stones, but he might find some buyers for big chunks of amethyst. He started to call back to

Emmet what he had found, until he spotted a gleaming yellow thread between layers of quartz and granite. His heart stopped. He moved closer.

Emmet's voice was faint. "What is it?"

It was too good to be true. Frank didn't want his initial thrill to be proven unfounded. It could be fool's gold.

As he reached out to touch the yellow trace, he knew there could be no question.

"Gold!" he called to Emmet.

"Gold?"

"Gold!" In the lantern light it seemed the vein of gold pulsed with the life of the earth. Joyous laughter bubbled out of him. "We found it! We found it!"

Tomorrow they would haul the equipment down here and start digging in earnest. His skin went as taut as a drumhead as he imagined the sensations of Mollie Hogan in his arms.

Emmet gave a hoot of joy.

The vein continued down into the darkness, drawing his attention into the deeper places, but this was enough for tonight. With renewed purpose and vigor, he turned back up toward their opening.

The change in perspective, however, revealed a branch in the cavern he had missed. A surge of curiosity gave him confidence he could follow this passage for a short distance without becoming lost, so he did.

A general incline of perhaps a fifty yards proved easy walking. What brought him up short was not Emmet's distant hollering but some things scattered over the floor that were not rocks.

Bones.

They formed an array, splintered and scattered, perhaps twenty feet across. In the exact center stood a strange shape, a sort of domed helmet with an upright fin down the center and a swooping brim, badly rusted. He stepped gingerly around ribs and long bones to reach the helmet where it lay at the center. He picked it up by the fin, and something clattered out and rolled against his foot.

A human skull.

Heart surging into his throat, he cried out and dropped the helmet, which banged to the stone with an echoing clang.

In the distance, Emmet hollered something Frank's ears couldn't catch.

Nearby lay a steel breastplate in a similar state of decay, leather straps and buckles eaten away by time.

About twenty feet farther up the passage, he spotted another helmet. Then another a bit farther on.

The more he looked around, however, the more he realized that the bones—the human ribs, the arm and leg bones—had been carefully arranged, the way a child might arrange sticks into a pattern on the ground. He could not fathom the image, but there was no mistake.

His former elation drained away, only to be replaced by cold, leaden dread.

"This looks like an old Spanish helmet," Emmet said. "Saw one in a picture book once." He turned the rusted helmet over and over.

Frank shivered at the memory of the way the skull sounded and felt when it hit his foot, hollow and dry.

"This must mean there's another entrance around here that we haven't found," Emmet said.

Frank shook his head and pointed down the mountain slope to the north, in the direction of the Georgetown camp. "I think it used to be over there, but whatever opening was there is gone. It was a solid cave-in."

They chewed quietly on hardtack and pemmican, ruminating, until darkness and chill descended and drove them into the warmer confines of their tent, where they soon bedded down for the night.

Frank's sleep was fitful as golden veins danced with bones in his fading imagination.

When he awoke, bright, silvery moonlight played through the tent flap. Sniffles let loose with a tremendous *heehaww* that sat Frank straight up on his cot. It was not like Sniffles to raise a ruckus at this time of night. Frank groped in the dark for the shotgun and hurried outside barefoot, wearing only his union suit.

The full moon cast silver dust over the mountainside, illuminating all in stark black and gray.

A deep, coarse sniffing sound near their crates of foodstuffs turned his bowels to water, and he turned slowly around expecting the shape of a bear rummaging through their supplies. Something was indeed hunched over one of the crates, sniffing.

He cocked both barrels of the shotgun. It was loaded with slugs for just this purpose; a load of buckshot would only put a bear in a pucker.

The click of the hammers brought the creature upright, but it wasn't a bear. It stood tall and thin like a man. An Injun in their camp counting coup? A tommy-knocker venturing out of its earthen home? "Hey, now, what are you doing there?" Frank said.

The figure's head swiveled to regard him, but kept swiveling like an owl's, cranking around an impossible degree to observe him, and its eyes gleamed like those of a night creature caught in the light. And there was something about the face that sent warm piss down the leg of Frank's union suit.

Slope-shouldered, forward slumped, and impossibly gaunt, with an unkempt shock of greasy hair atop a pointed head. Its legs bent backwards like a dog's.

Frank cried out Emmet's name, spasms in his fingers squeezing both triggers. The double explosion jerked the shotgun muzzle high, and orange sparks and thick smoke exploded into the night.

The thing dropped to all fours, snatched something on the ground with long, clawed fingers, and charged toward the mine entrance, dragging a substantial burden as if it weighed nothing.

"Emmet" Frank cried again. "Get out here!"

The black mouth of the mine entrance swallowed the creature and its burden.

Emmet didn't come out of the tent.

"Emmet!"

19

Frank had once seen a chimpanzee in a zoo run on all fours like that. Circling to the tent flap, he opened it, and the moonlight revealed Emmet's empty cot.

His sleep-addled mind registered the two limp, flopping arms disappearing into blackness.

He ran to the mine entrance. "Emmet!"

In the distance, the sounds of something dragging over the planks covering the shaft floor diminished.

⟐

His hands trembled so badly he could barely hold the match to the lantern wick. He jumped into his trousers and boots, and reloaded their father's shotgun, hands fumbling more powder onto the ground than down the barrels. As he fumbled, images of those lantern eyes and a protuberant snout flashed in his mind's eye. He set the tin onto the head of the powder barrel and jammed wadding and slug into each barrel.

Emmet would know what to do, he always had, but he was gone. Frank was the elder, but Emmet possessed the hardier temperament. How could Frank return to Baltimore and tell their mother he'd let Emmet get eaten by some strange beast? As an added precaution for light, he lit the wick and thrust his mining hat onto his head, then stuffed his pockets with candles.

With a deep shuddering breath, lantern in one hand, shotgun tucked under the other armpit, he hurried into the shaft.

Of course it looked no different in the dead of night, but something about the hour still sent cold spiders crawling up his neck.

"Emmet! I'm coming!" he shouted into the black.

That thing had moved with a speed that further unnerved him. How could he ever catch it?

As he ran, the bobbing lantern cast a dizzying array of shifting shadows on the rough-hewn stone walls and wooden supports, a feeble globe of blessed illumination with him at the center.

A dark, wet smear appeared on the floor planks.

"Emmet!" he cried.

He reached the opening into the cavern, finding more blood smeared on the rough stone. He slung the shotgun over his back. The rope and hook seemed secure, but he was forced to douse the lantern and hook it to his belt to keep both hands free to lower himself inside. With rope in hand he stuffed himself feet-first through the opening, half-expecting some rubbery black claw to seize him by the ankle and drag him into the earth's bowels like Emmet.

As he set his feet upon the cavern floor, the blackness pressed in around him like cold water, as if the air itself was thickening. His heartbeat was the only thing he could hear as he re-lit the lantern.

Calling Emmet's name, he set off into the deeper blackness, hanging the lantern from his shotgun barrel to keep the gun at the ready.

Deeper he went than before, through caverns and passages that narrowed and expanded, twisted and turned, following blood smears, dreading the moment when he might encounter something larger than a smear.

An hour must have passed by the time the blood smears petered out. How deep he had come, he had no notion. A mile? Two? He had moved expeditiously, hoping to catch the creature and yet fearing the moment of confrontation. How much oil remained in his lantern? In his hat lamp? He doused the hat lamp, chiding himself for not realizing that he might need both to get himself out of here. With the candles, he had at least a day's worth of light, but if it all ran out, he would be left with only a handful of matches and nothing else to burn. He turned the wick down to its lowest level to conserve fuel, leaving him only a tiny guttering flame by which to see.

Another hour passed. Each step deeper made him yearn for another spot of his brother's blood to lead him on. He couldn't turn back. Not now. Not even if he found a whole nest of those things.

But he was growing weary. He quenched his thirst from a trickle of wetness on a cavern wall. It tasted awful, chalky, but it wet his tongue.

The edge of his circle of light had grown so nebulous, his eyes so bleary, that he almost walked straight into the yawning abyss that opened before him.

His feet teetered on the edge, arms windmilling as he fought for balance. In the lantern's flailing arcs, the flame went out, plunging him into profound blackness. He fell back on the floor, gasping for breath, lantern clattering beside him. He was not a praying man, but he now thanked the Almighty with everything he had.

He lay there for a moment, regathering his wits, his vision blacker than if his eyes were closed. After a time, he became aware of a sickly, greenish blue glow casting shadows on the ceiling, emanating from the abyss.

Rolling onto his belly, he inched forward, feeling for the precipice. He peered over the edge into a cavern vast beyond comprehension, painted with light on walls and structures. Towers and buttresses, catwalks and spires, minarets and pylons, all limned in swaths of blue-green algae. Odd angles induced a dizziness he could not blink away.

From the depths came peculiar meeping, mewling, whispers.

Black specks moved across the blue-green tapestries like ants.

Distant whispers echoed up to him, but the voices were so guttural that he couldn't be sure they were speaking words at all.

"...what is it..."

"...a long time since we have..."

"...juicy..."

Snatches of other languages interspersed what he heard, Spanish, some heathen Chinese and Injun tongues, all intermixed with that peeping, meeping, mewling.

"...fresh meat on the foot out there..."

"...too fresh..."

"...no more eating worms and algae..."

"...too long below..."

A sudden sniffing sound like he had heard in camp, but right on top of him, yanked a gasp out of him. He scrambled away from the lip of the abyss. One flailing hand brushed something cold and rubbery. The other arm brushed the lantern, sending it clattering over the edge and into the void. Time stretched into eternity before the lantern struck anything, impossibly distant. Cold breath brushed the stench of foetor and blood across his cheek.

His hand closed over the shotgun. In the faint glow, a nebulous, low-slung shape shifted its stance, regarding him. With a ragged, rasping cry, he raised the shotgun, cocking both hammers. The muzzle flash blinded him again with no reckoning of whether he'd hit it. The cavern's confines redoubled the report, blasting a faint, muffled whine into his ears and masking all other sound. The acrid stench of powder smoke filled his nose, along with something pungent and sickly, the stench of the grave.

He flung himself away from the void, back up the passage, relying on his memory to take him as far as it could from the lip of that awful abyss.

Stopping to listen for pursuit, he fumbled out a match to light his hat lamp.

The mewling, meeping chorus grew louder, lending frantic speed to his heels.

Running in the opposite direction altered his perspective so profoundly he would have been lost immediately if not for Emmet's blood trail. Without his brother's blood, he would be a dead man.

For at least a mile he ran, up, up, around, ducking and climbing and squeezing, each breath like a strip of lung being raked out.

At the top of a vaulted galley, curtained by sheets of wavy, nacreous stone, he paused to look back. Well outside the feeble sphere of his hat lamp's glow, lantern-like eyes hovered in the blackness, some standing high, some slinking low, regarding him as he regarded them.

Given the alacrity with which the first creature had dragged his brother away, they could have long since brought him down like wolves on a wounded elk.

But these wolves were playing with him, curious about him, thoughtful, calculating.

He ran on, praying for his hat lamp to stay alive. For at least two more miles he ran and stumbled and gasped and wept, up and up, round and round.

Behind came that damnable noise, like the sound of demonic infants speaking their own language.

What sounded like Emmet's voice reached out to him from behind, washing like a shipwreck from the tide of infernal noise, calling Frank's name. "Stop...wait...want to see..." The sound of it made him pause.

But it couldn't be Emmet. Emmet was dead, and they were picking their teeth with his bones.

And other voices. "...fear makes it tender, it does..."

"...juicier..."

"...dash out its brains..."

"...hang it to ripen..."

"...slurp out its veins..."

On and on, he ran, praying for deliverance. Surely he had stumbled on a portal to Hell.

The creatures had been trapped in the earth for untold centuries, millennia. Ever since the Spaniards found them and collapsed the entrance to this underworld.

What would these monsters do if they got loose? They would find plenty of unsuspecting prey in the Georgetown camp and among the lone prospectors dotting the mountainsides.

They would find beautiful, sweet, kind Mollie, sleeping in her tent, helpless in the black of night.

That was when he knew what he had to do.

❧

The rope still hung where he had left it. In the endless flight, moments of doubt had plagued him. The sight of it sent fresh vigor coursing through him and he hit the rope like a climbing monkey.

As he climbed, the presences behind him closed in.

The muzzle of the shotgun slung across his shoulders caught against the hole's rim. He struggled to draw it in. Lantern eyes gleamed with the light of his hat lamp.

Finally with a shrill curse, he shrugged the shotgun off and let it fall, then jammed himself through the opening, tearing furrows in his skin. He gasped for the fresh air of the upper world and flung himself upward. Primal instinct urged him to flee into the night and not look back. But the creatures would find him. Even if he reached Georgetown, no one would believe him. Out here, there was no law, no cavalry.

He burst into the moonlight, giving Sniffles a start. The burro regarded him with sleepy indifference as he seized the rim of the barrel of powder they used for blasting. No strength remained in his arms save that of desperation. The half-full barrel, centered under the slide, where the shaft was most unstable, should be sufficient to collapse the shaft.

He shoved the barrel over and rolled it into the tunnel, his muscles like limp steaks.

He met them sixty feet inside. They slunk along the floor, clung like bats to the roof beams, their claws scratching the rock and their eyes like dying lanterns.

"...it has the powder..."

"...like the others..."

"...seize it..."

"...gouge its flesh..."

"...*cometelo*..."

"...*yao ta*..."

"...twist its neck..."

"...chew it..."

"...*masticalo*..."

"...*dapo gutou*..."

"...*tekeli-li...tekeli-li*..."

"...wait, the powder!"

Twisted, once-human faces took shape in the guttering light, hungry, slavering, splintered yellow teeth in elongated snouts, noses shrunk to slits, pointed ears sticking from mops of greasy black hair, skin bruise-black and rubbery, long arms, long fingers tipped with black talons.

They poised less than twenty feet from him. He had no fuse.

He righted the barrel, glanced over his shoulder for one last look at the moonlight, and thought of Mollie's lips as he struck the match.

꩜

TRAVIS HEERMANN

Freelance writer, novelist, award-winning screen-writer, editor, poker player, poet, biker, roustabout, **Travis Heermann** is a graduate of the Odyssey Writing Workshop and the author of *The Ronin Trilogy, The Wild Boys, Rogues of the Black Fury,* and co-author of *Death Wind,* plus short fiction pieces in anthologies and magazines such as *Apex Magazine, Alembical,* the *Fiction River* anthology series, *Historical Lovecraft,* and Cemetery Dance's *Shivers VII.* As a freelance writer, he has produced a metric ton of role-playing game work both in print and online, including the *Firefly Roleplaying Game, Battletech, Legend of Five Rings, d20 System,* and the MMORPG, EVE Online.

He enjoys cycling, martial arts, torturing young minds with otherworldly ideas, and zombies. He has three long-cherished dreams: a produced screenplay, a NYT best-seller, and a seat in the World Series of Poker.

In 2016, he returned to the U.S. after living in New Zealand for a year with his family, toting more Middle Earth souvenirs and photos than is reasonable.

THE SILVER BELLE

BETSY DORNBUSCH

1875
COLORADO TERRITORY

An undercurrent of voices filled the gaps between the random pounding of dozens of hammers as I stepped down from the coach. Music spilled out onto the dusty street from a saloon a few doors down. The air smelled of crisp pine. The sun's heat prickled my brow before I put my hat back on.

I stretched my back and picked up my bag for the short walk across the road to the hotel the driver indicated was mine. It was no Barton House Hotel, where President Grant recently stayed, but the windows shone and the pale gold paint was fresh. A crisp sign announced its name: *Hotel de Paris.* Run by an educated French miner who'd turned hotelier, I'd been told, but we'd see about that. Men came from all over and I'd learned not to trust them at first sniff.

I glanced up at the sky. It rained near every afternoon in the mountains and today looked to be no different. I didn't mind. Cooled the air, and tempers, too.

The hotel dampened the sounds of the voices and hammers. A man, impressively mustached, met me at the door. "Welcome, sir. Welcome. Come in. You are Mr. Cook?"

His accent was French and his tone courteous. I made a note of it. Courtesy was always of aid when investigating murder.

I gave him a nod but held my smile in reserve. "I am, indeed, thank you. And you must be Mr. Dupuy. Mrs. Hackett told you I was arriving today, I trust."

"Oui, sir." Dupuy put my name and address in the register and told me the hours for dinner. "Up the steps, to the right. Mrs. Gally will take you." He took a room key off the rack of twenty and offered it to me.

The room was clean and spare, the furniture very fine. I set my case on the floor and washed my face in the marble basin with two taps, one even warm. Impressive accommodations for the mountains, but silver bought the finer things in life and Georgetown was flush with it. I carried my hat back downstairs and asked to speak to Dupuy. He led me into a large room lined with chest-high bookshelves.

"This is very impressive." I meant it.

"I enjoy my books." Dupuy gave a self-depreciating smile and offered me a seat. Mrs. Gally carried in a tray with coffee. She didn't speak to me, though she and Dupuy exchanged a few words in French.

"I expect you know why I'm here," I said.

"Poor Annabelle," Dupuy said. "She is fortunate to have the Rocky Mountain Detective Agency overseeing her case. Your reputation is very good."

"Good fortune come too late, but thank you just the same. You knew Miss Shine." Not her real name, of course.

"Well acquainted for a time, less so right before her death."

Miss Shine had been a dancer, so I assumed their acquaintanceship was of a business nature, the sort conducted during evening hours. "Why less so?" I asked. The Frenchman was strapping and charming, if a little old for the likes of Miss Shine.

"She was leaving the saloon," Dupuy said pleasantly. "She was in love."

"I see. With who?"

A delicate shrug. "I do not know. She did not tell me."

"Do you have any idea who might have killed her?"

"I am sure I do not."

"Hazard a guess?"

Dupey spread his hands. "She had found someone she loved and turned her back on her admirers. So the killer must be one of her jilted lovers, perhaps?"

"Do you count yourself among them?"

"Oh, no. I am in love with someone else."

"Ah. Congratulations?"

He sighed sadly. "Would that she loved me back. Will you go see the sheriff now?"

"I thought to."

"He chases thieves today but surely will return by nightfall."

I got to my feet. "Thanks for the tip."

"Mr. Cook, there is one other thing you should know about Miss Shine… Annabelle." He smoothed his hand over his perfectly clean trouser leg. "She is supposedly a ghost about town. The men see her on the roads by the miner's cabins, and the saloon where she danced late at night, and the firehouse."

"The firehouse?"

"It's what the lads say. They are up all night, and sober, too."

I had no call to insult the man's intelligence. He was well-read and worldly. But he'd brought it up. "You believe in ghosts, Mr. Dupuy?"

"Such things are beyond me, but the miners believe. And beliefs can be the making of a man."

Or his undoing. "I'll bear that in mind."

I strolled in a light rain down Sixth Street, gazing in the windows and doors of new dry goods shops, hardware stores, and confectionaries, tipping my hat to a few smiling ladies. People seemed friendly enough, if collectively from a half dozen different places in the world. Louis Dupuy's accent didn't stick out so much here. I turned onto Brownell Street, where Mrs. Leta Hackett, my client, ran the Silver Mountain Saloon.

I stepped inside, casting a wary eye. I didn't have to worry though; the place was mostly empty. The bartender wiped his spectacles. He put them on and peered at me. A woman in a burgundy dress spoke to him, her back to me and the door, and a lone drunk propped on his elbow over an empty glass. About what I'd expect before dinner. Before the miners climbed out of the deep earth to spend their hard dug silver on whiskey and dancing and more.

The woman turned and came forward. While the skirts behind nearly brushed the floor, the ruffled front had been hemmed up to her knees, and scooped nearly to the top of her corset. I took off my hat, keeping my gaze firmly on her face. "Mrs. Hackett?"

The drunk lifted his head and looked at me. His shirt was dirty, his jacket dusty.

As she lit up with a welcoming smile, I saw then how she must do so well in her business. "Mr. Cook. You look like your picture in the newspaper. Come in. May I offer you a whiskey?"

"Maybe later, ma'am. I'll keep a clear head for now." I sat where she bid me. As she gestured to the bartender, I braced myself for my second coffee in as many hours and a long evening of wakefulness. "Have you learned anything new since you telegraphed me?"

"Someone came forward. One of the fire lads. Jacob Hurd is his name. He thanked me for helping find her killer." She paused. "He didn't say as much but I think he must have been her lover. Maybe even fiancé. She was leaving the saloon."

That explained the "sightings" at the firehouse. I wondered who knew about Jacob Hurd and Annabelle Shine, and if there really was more to it than rumor or wishful thinking on his part. "To marry him?"

"It's our biggest means of attrition," she said.

"Did Miss Shine make a good living in the saloon?"

She smiled. "She was beautiful and kind. She liked the men, Mr. Cook, and they liked her."

"I imagine Mr. Hurd might not have appreciated their mutual affection."

"He didn't kill her, if that's what you're implying."

I sighed. "If you're so certain, then why am I here, Mrs. Hackett?"

"Because I think he knows who did."

Jacob Hurd lived in a little cabin in a row of identical structures on the outskirts of town. Getting there made for a nice walk in the early summer evening, and no one was drunk enough yet to try to tangle with me. I found it odd he'd got his own cabin to himself on a fire lad's wages, but maybe he worked it out with Annabelle, if they were to be married. I banged on his door but got no answer. The shutters were latched up. I stood on the little wooden step and looked around, holding my hat.

A familiar man appeared in the doorway to the cabin next door. He leaned in it, smoking.

"I saw you in Mrs Hackett's saloon," I said. "I don't mind saying I thought you were right drunk."

"I can handle my liquor."

"A man not working, drinking in the daylight hours, usually means something's wrong." I smiled in a friendly fashion, showing I meant no insult to him. "I'm David

Cook with the Rocky Mountain Detective Agency. You?"

He studied me a long moment before admitting, "Clay Slade."

"Know anything about where Jacob Hurd might be, Mr. Slade?"

"Ain't seen him for a few days."

"Do you usually?"

"When he's not at the firehouse."

"You're certain that's not where he is now?"

"No, he told me he had a couple of days off. Something to do with some woman."

I turned to regard the closed door. Rattled the knob, but it was locked. On a hunch, I leaned toward a crack in it and sniffed. My nose wrinkled at the familiar scent: the sickly-sweet, cold air of death. Maybe he'd got some game in there turned rank. Hardly seemed likely for a man about to bring his bride home. Or… I put my shoulder to the door, hard.

"Hey!" Slade cried, trotting over, but I was already inside and shaking my head.

"That him?" I asked.

Slade swallowed, staring. "It's him. It's Jake."

Jake. Maybe they were better friends than Slade let on. "Best fetch the sheriff, Mr. Slade."

Clay Slade wasn't going to be running off for the sheriff right away any more than Jacob Hurd was going to be telling me who killed Annabelle Shine. The first was busy being sick in the dirt outside, and the latter was busy being dead from a bullet wound to the chest.

❧

Not much of note about the body but a nasty hole on one side, a bigger hole on the other, and the thick, sweet smell of dried blood and decomposing body. The sheriff agreed he must've died right quick. He thanked me for my help, told me my reputation preceded me, and hinted that I should've come around to see him before seeing anyone else.

"Thanks. You were on my list but I got word you were out of town. Catch those thieves?"

The sheriff said he had.

"I reckon you saw Annabelle Shine's body after she died?"

The sheriff had, and found nothing missing from her room. Strangled with two hands, the marks clear as day on her white throat. Face looked pretty as ever. Barely mussed her rouged cheeks. She fought back though; broke a nail clawing at whoever had done it to her.

A week on, those scratches might still be on the man who killed her. "And no suspects?"

"Nothing. It was like a ghost had come and done it."

"What about this one?" I pointed at the more recently dead body on the floor.

The sheriff shook his head. Hurd had a good reputation as a hard worker. And no, he didn't know Jacob Hurd loved Miss Shine, but he wasn't surprised. She was Annabelle Shine. Who didn't?

I'd meant if the sheriff had any idea who'd killed Jacob Hurd, but I let it go. I'd figure it out myself. After they photographed the body and carried it out, along with most of the stink, I started pulling things apart: the crockery down from shelves, the mattress off the bed. I frowned and bent to cut it open, wondering if I'd find bank notes or something else hidden, but a lump of fabric under the floor in the corner caught my eye. I stepped through the ropes of the bed frame to grab it.

It was a canvas bag, heavier than it looked. I hefted it up to the lantern and smoothed the thick fabric. *Miners National Bank est. 1874.* I undid the ties and pulled out what felt like a palm-sized rough stone. It was dark grey but glimmered silver in the lantern light.

I whistled low and showed it to the sheriff. "What do you make of that?"

"Looks like Jacob Hurd stole some silver ore. Pretty good motive for his killing. A sorry coincidence he died before you got to him."

I wasn't so sure. Coincidence wasn't a belief that shaped me.

❧

When I returned to see Mrs. Hackett later that evening, the Silver Mountain Saloon was filled with miners and dancing ladies. She was easy to find; she watched all that went on from her place at the bar, a crystal glass of sherry at her elbow.

"I heard about Jacob," she said by way of greeting, and led me to a back room with a desk and account books neatly lining the shelves of a bookcase. She sat at her desk in an upholstered chair and indicated I take its mate.

I'd previously decided not to go into too much detail. "Jacob Hurd had some silver ore hidden under his bed."

She frowned, fine lines around her mouth betraying her as further along in age than I'd thought. "How would he come by it? He never went near the mines."

"Right. Maybe he's involved with someone else stealing silver, or someone gave it to him. Have you heard rumors of silver being stolen directly from the mines?"

"No. I wouldn't have, though. Perhaps some of the girls… or Buck is here. He might know."

"Buck?"

A wry smile. "Francis Buckner, the first shift mine boss. Makes the men call him 'The Buck.' If silver is going missing at the mines, he'll know. I'll fetch him for you."

I didn't have to wait long. Francis Buckner was just starting go thin on top and had a booming voice that didn't match his average frame. A yellow vest shone against his white shirt and dark coat. He gripped my hand too tight by my reckoning. I waited for him to prove his superior manhood to himself and then sat him down in the guest chair while I took Mrs. Hackett's. "Thanks for talking to me, Mr. Buckner."

"They call me the Buck. Ya got news on some stolen silver?"

"I'm investigating Miss Annabelle Shine's murder and found what I think might be some stolen silver."

"How much?"

I held out my hands to show him the size of the bag. "Give or take. Heavy, though."

"Where'd ya find it?"

"Do you know anything about some stolen silver, Mr Buckner?"

He pursed his lips. They shone a bit with spittle or sweat. "There's no way to smuggle that much silver out of the mine. The men are checked as they come out. They might get away with a rock or two but no more than that at one time."

I kept my face still. "I didn't say it was from the mine."

"Where else would it be from, if you're askin' me?"

He was quick on his feet. I had to give him that. "Jacob Hurd was a fire lad."

"That's right."

"Do you know him?"

"Met a time or two."

"Here?"

Another shrug. "Maybe. Or about town."

"He's dead."

A pause. "That's a shame."

"Did you ever see Annabelle Shine? Dance with her?"

"Sure. A lot of men did."

"Frequently?"

"I'm not sure what ya mean by *frequently*."

"How often did you spend time with Miss Shine?"

"At least weekly. Sometimes more. She was a sweet girl. Knew how to please a man." Buckner glanced around like he heard something. Caught the edges of his jacket in his hands and tugged them a little tighter over his yellow vest. It was getting chilly in the backroom since the day's heat had worn off. I felt a draft on the back of my neck.

"You quit seeing her before she died?"

Buckner shrugged. "Later than some, but yeah. I quit her two weeks ago."

"Her idea or yours?"

He just looked at me.

"Maybe she got tired of saying no. Gave you some lip over it."

"Not just me," he said, indignant. "She wasn't dancing no more."

"Few weeks ago is about the time she took up with some man, isn't it? Maybe a month?"

"If ya say so."

"I'm asking, not telling, Mr. Buckner."

"It's what I hear."

So he'd kept asking her to be with him after she'd quit dancing. For at least a week, maybe two. Persistent man.

"Who was the lucky man?" I asked him. "Jacob Hurd?"

His lips twitched. "I don't know. There were some rumors."

"Where were you the night Miss Shine was strangled?" I let my gaze fall pointedly to his hands.

"I was at home."

"Alone?"

"Felt poorly. My housekeeper might've seen me. I forget."

Convenient. "You ever get any silver ore as a bonus for being the shift boss?"

40

"Not for a while." He eased forward, body and booted feet intruding on my space. "I just want bank notes. It's easier now National Miner's come to town."

"How long you been mining in Colorado Territory, Mr. Buckner?"

"Since Sixty-Three."

"And at the Belmont Lode?"

"Almost since it was found."

Eighteen-Sixty-Four, then, or a bit after. "That's a long time. You got a few bags of silver ore sitting around somewhere, I reckon. From before the bank came to town. A smart man would set it aside for a rainy day."

"I reckon I do. More money in the bank though."

"Ever have any trouble with the law, Mr. Buckner?"

His jaw jutted out. "None."

"I want to see your wrists, if I might."

His nostrils flared. I knew he was considering saying no. I waited. I had a lot of practice at it. He shoved up his sleeves and showed me. No scratches to speak of... nothing a miner wouldn't't have. Maybe he'd worn gloves.

"Is that all?" he asked, his tone booming and sharp.

"For now, thanks."

He shoved his hat on his head and stalked through the crowd, bumping elbows and shoulders like the men and dancers got in his way on purpose. I reckoned he'd be counting those bags of silver of his soon, and I reckoned I'd best follow. As I went to the door, I saw Clay Slade leaning against the bar watching us go.

I lost Buckner almost immediately. Brownell Street was busy with miners, saloons, and brothels, and a moonless darkness had descended over Georgetown. Light from doorways and windows barely penetrated it. I reckoned I'd go back to Hotel de Paris and get some shut-eye. It had been a long day and tomorrow would be longer.

The streets quieted a block away from Brownell, where the shops were shut up for the night. Gaslights from the hotel glowed at the other end of the street but I had a long patch of darkness to walk through. I rested my hand on my revolver and kept my eyes up and moving all around as I walked, but I didn't really expect trouble. A couple of times I thought I heard steps behind me but when I glanced back I was alone. Then two blocks down at Rose Street a fleeting grey shadow caught my eye. I found myself slowing as I tried to pick it out from the darkness, and by the time I hit the corner of the boardwalk I stopped. My head prickled under my hat, but with chill, not heat.

A female shape stood in the middle of the street, staring at me, shadowed in the night. Later I realized I shouldn't have been able to see her at all. Not one gaslight burned down there and the moon still hid behind the mountains. But I did see her. Her dress was silvery-grey, and her hair piled up on her head was too. Her skin looked pale, like she'd never seen the sun.

"Miss? Do you need help?" I called, squinting.

She lifted a hand toward me, I thought I heard her soft voice, then she turned and walked in the other direction.

I stared a moment before following. Anyone who knew Annabelle and Mrs. Hackett would know I was in town investigating the murder, and I could think of plenty of reasons why a witness… particularly a female witness… would want to speak to me secretly. The most important being that my first real lead I'd found shot dead.

But she didn't stop. She kept on walking, getting further ahead and keeping that way no matter how quick I followed.

"Miss," I called, trying to keep my voice down. "Wait."

But she paid me no mind as she led me out of town and into the woods. Her grey form flickered through the trees. The moon emerged from behind the mountain, and I thought for a moment she *disappeared* into the light, which ought to be the opposite of what happened to a body.

The night chill deepened in my bones. "No one will see us here, miss."

But she kept on walking until she just… *didn't* anymore. The trees swallowed her up. This time she really was gone. Not a whisper of boot on the ground; not a swoosh of skirts against foliage.

I stopped, stunned, and looked all around. "Miss?"

Nothing. Silence, more silent than the woods ought to be.

Sweat stung my back despite the cold mountain night. I loosed my revolver in its holster and walked in a circle, expecting someone to jump me at any moment. Nothing flew or climbed or slithered through the trees. No wind. That struck me most of all. Not a breath of air moved the pine boughs. Chills crawled up and down my spine.

As the moon emerged from behind a cloud, a square black shadow appeared almost hidden amid more trees. I moved that way, easing my gun out. An old mine entrance? No… a pile of cut stones with a lone, dark log wall leaning against some trees. The ruins to an old cabin, lit by the moon through the clearing. I stepped "inside" the structure, looking around. A hump of trash filled one low corner. When it didn't move, I nudged it with my boot, still expecting something to jump out at me.

I might as well have tried to nudge the wall itself, the mound was that unmovable. I knelt and pulled part of it to me. A bag. It made a rough scraping sound inside, like rocks… they spilled out from the drawstring top, glimmering in my hand. I spread out the bag to read. It was from National Miner's Bank. I'd found a stash of silver ore, a big one.

On a hunch I put the ore and bag back and moved into the shadow of the trees where I could see inside the ruins but no one could see me. I settled in to wait. My joints were stiffening from the cold, and I was about to give up the wait as downright foolishness when a dark, hatted figure appeared. Whoever he was—I could see that much when he entered the moonlit ruins—bent to check the bags of ore. He was there what felt like a long while, shifting them. Counting, most like.

Then he rose and stretched, hands on the small of his back. His hat still shadowed his face but his jacket parted to reveal a yellow silk vest.

44

I'm smart enough not to arrest a man in the middle of the woods at night. After Buckner left, I waited a good while before trudging back toward town and my hotel, certain of my man. Buckner had possible motive for killing Jacob Hurd, and the sort of temperament that could drive him to kill an uncooperative dancing girl.

Louis Dupuy was awake and waiting for me, reading in his library. I poked my head in. "Thanks for leaving the place unlocked for me. Sorry I'm so late."

"The law never sleeps, Mr. Cook."

"The law might, but the criminals sure don't."

"Will you take a drink?"

"I would, and glad of it, sir."

He poured out whiskey and we sat companionably.

"Do you know Mr. Buckner?" I asked.

"Oui. He used to be my boss. In the mines."

"You gave it up for this?" I gestured to the hotel around us.

"I was injured."

Looking at him straight on, I could see faint scarring around his left eye. It matched the apparent stiffness I'd seen earlier. "I see. Good man?"

"Not a bad man. But too … *épris*, no, no…enamored of himself. Always trying to insist he is worthy of our respect. Demanding it. Do you take my meaning?"

"I do at that." I sipped my whiskey. "And the ladies? What do they think of him?"

He snorted softly and held up his thumb and finger an inch apart. "*Petit, petit,* they say. I do not know if their gossip is true. The ladies, they tease the men. But Mr. Buckner is not a man for such teasing."

"I expect not," I said.

I went to bed, watching the moon out my window and thinking things over. It had fallen all too clear: Buckner asked Annabelle to take him to bed again, she refused. He insisted; unaccustomed to refusal when he demanded his way. Perhaps she made fun of him, hoping to make him go away. Instead, the man with the *petit* confidence had attacked her, hands around her throat, demanding she apologize.

But she couldn't take the words back; she was dead.

Footsteps came down the hall. The hotel had been sleeping when I arrived and Dupuy had locked the door when we went to bed. Someone up for the toilet, maybe.

But they stopped outside my door.

I frowned and got up to open it. "Can I help y—" I blinked and looked down the hall both ways. No one was there.

I shut the door and went back to bed. There, resting on my white linen pillow, were three pieces of silver ore glimmering in the moonlight. I don't mind admitting that I didn't sleep any more that night.

❧

Buckner would be at the mine for his shift. He had no reason to think I was planning to arrest him for murdering Annabelle Shine. But I still had one loose end, and that was Jacob Hurd. Why had he been killed? Was it because he had stolen silver ore from Buckner's stash? Or had the ore been a payout of some sort? Or had it to do with Annabelle's murder? Buckner admitted he and Hurd knew each other. There was no real proof Hurd had been with Annabelle the night she died, and Buckner had been vague enough to raise my hackles. I went back to talk to Hurd's neighbors again, particularly his friend Clay Slade. Perhaps someone along the road had seen something that would lead to Hurd's killer, and then Annabelle's.

There was a bit of scrambling inside at my knock. Slade opened the door. He was unshaven, hair greasy and unkempt.

"You look like hell, Mr. Slade. Are you ill, hungover or exhausted?"

His lips tightened. Thin already, they nearly disappeared. "What do you want?"

"I have more questions for you."

"I told you everything I know."

"Sometimes the littlest thing matters. You'd be surprised. Can I come in?" I already had my boot in the way of the door so I pushed past him. "Thanks."

The shut up house was hot and rank, stinking of unwashed body and trash and old cigarette smoke. I glanced around but saw nothing out of line with the house of an out-of-work, drunken bachelor. "I have to say, I find yours and Mr. Hurd's friendship an odd one."

"We were neighbors, that's all."

"Really? I heard you were pretty close." A lie, but lies usually stacked up like a house of cards over the truth. One more could bring the whole thing down.

"From who?"

I walked over to his stove and scrutinized the rusty cast iron skillet with hardened scraps of egg stuck to it. "Seems a nice cabin for a man out of work, though it could use a good scrubbing."

"I told you, I was a miner."

"Fired?"

"I already earned enough to get by."

"Most men, they earn their fortune and let it take them somewhere else more comfortable. Denver, even." I rubbed the back of my neck as a cooler breeze touched it, my senses telling me I might be onto something.

"What do you want?"

"I want to know how Mr. Hurd came to be dead a few short weeks after his girl ended up murdered. I want to know how that silver ore got in his cabin. I want to know who is at the bottom of it, and why." I paused. "What do you know of Francis Buckner?"

Slade blinked. "Buck? I worked for him for a while."

"How'd he know Jacob Hurd?"

"I don't know. Jake kept his own business quiet."

"Did Buckner ever hire Miss Shine?" A breath of surety ran down my spine, but it had me antsy too. I held still, covering. No use in showing it.

His head twitched no. "How would I know?"

"How indeed, Mr. Slade. Did you ever hire her?"

He chewed the inside of his lip. "Lots of men did—"

"I ain't asking about them, now am I? I'm asking about you." I paused to wait for an answer. When none came, I said, "Mrs. Hackett seems a capable type. I was in her office. Big ole shelves with stacks of accounting books in there. I imagine a woman like that has records dating back to the opening of the Silver Mountain Saloon. Of course, I won't need to go back that far. I reckon I can go back to the week or two before some man strangled the life from beautiful, sweet Annabelle Shine."

I rubbed the back of my neck. For a hot, shut up little cabin, I couldn't for the life of me reckon where a cool draft came from. It had grown into a real chill, not just my usual detective ability making its talent known.

I dug in my pocket and held out the pieces of silver ore. "These look familiar, Mr. Slade?"

He had every reason to mock the question. He was a miner. Instead he stared at me. His thin lips parted. A faint glimmer shone in his eyes, though from where, I didn't know because the cabin was only lit by the sun muted by dusty calico curtains. He darted to one side, toward his bed. No, the table by it. I yanked my gun from its holster but a silver blur was quicker. Like a slender cloud, a silvery form raced at and through Slade. He shouted and shuddered and dropped like a bag of grain off a jolting wagon.

I blinked, doing my share of staring myself. The silvery form of a woman stood over Slade. She pointed at him, and then under the bed. But I couldn't make my mind think what she meant by it. I just stared, picking out details. The fine curve of her cheek, a peek of shapely calf under her short, ruffled skirts. Her determined expression. The table and wall through her hazy form.

"Annabelle," I said.

She just pointed again at Slade, and then under the bed.

I detected a hint of impatience on her part. My mind snapped back into life. I blinked.

Annabelle was gone. Heat descended onto the cabin, pressing on my skin and lungs. Half-sick from the oppressive air, I bent down to pull out three bank bags, heavy with silver ore.

Slade was stirring. I grabbed his arms and clipped my trusty Adams handcuffs on him, taking the opportunity to pull up his sleeves. His forearms were scratched to hell. He moaned.

I strode to the door to throw it open. The room was stuffy and stinking, all the ghostly chill gone with Annabelle.

Slade seemed to come-to a bit. He mumbled, "She won't leave me alone."

No wonder the man looked like hell. I squatted by him and set the pieces of silver ore where he could see them. "If you don't tell me what this is about, she'll only keep coming back."

"Jake stole the ore, not me. He left the bag right out in his cabin, dang fool. I told him he'd better hide it or he'd get caught. I didn't mean nothing by it. I was just joking. But he took it wrong and he threatened me. Roughed me up over it. Since it was that worthwhile I told him I wanted in. I wanted some silver. If I was in on it, I wouldn't talk. After we took some more, I told him he'd best say nothing to no one, especially once I worked out it was Buck's stash. Buck'd see us hanged if he found out. But the fool loved Annabelle. Wanted to marry her. So he told her. And that's when he found out she didn't love him back." He swallowed, hard. "She said she'd keep quiet but Buck kept bugging her for one last night. We all knew he was doing that. So I reckoned she'd tell him what we done to distract him, just to get him to leave her be. I couldn't let her do that."

A silence as I studied him. "And Jake?"

"He wasn't doing so good after she was gone. I tried to tell him she was never his to cry over anyway, but he acted crazy. I had to shut him up. He was going to ruin the whole thing."

❧

"I want to thank you for your hospitality," I told Dupuy before carrying my bag across the street where the coach back to Denver waited.

He shook his head a little and gave me a bemused smile. "It is remarkable, your solving this mystery for us, Mr. Cook. The town of Georgetown is in your debt. But how did you do it?"

I almost told him what I told everybody clsc when they asked me the same question: *I like it. I can't help it; it is natural.* But I hadn't done the work on my own. "This is a real friendly town. I had a lot of good help."

51

Dupuy gave me a speculative look. "Sheriff says Mr. Slade is half-mad, ranting about the ghost of Annabelle Shine over in the jail. He says even you saw her?"

I thought about Annabelle. She'd done what she needed: led me to her lover's killer, and her own. I doubted she'd bother anyone again. "If there's any good fortune to dying, Mr. Dupuy, it's getting to rest in peace. I have every hope Annabelle Shine will now."

I tipped my hat to the Frenchman and climbed back into the stagecoach back to Denver.

⁓

BETSY DORNBUSCH

Betsy Dornbusch is the author of several fantasy short stories, novellas, and novels, including the *Books of the Seven Eyes* trilogy and *The Silver Scar*, which is forthcoming from Night Shade Books in 2018. When she's not writing or speaking at conventions, she reads, snowboards, and goes to concerts. Betsy and her family split their time between Boulder and Grand Lake, Colorado.

A BOUQUET OF WONDER AND MARVEL

SEAN EADS

1882

The Leadville miners, the painted ladies at the bar, and even the piano player laughed at Benson, waving the check in the air and begging again for help.

"We're all rich here. *Metal* rich. No one cares about the promises of a slip of paper."

"It's your Christian duty to help a neighbor. Georgetown is in trouble!"

More sneers showed Benson the futility of his efforts—until the check was pinched out of his grip. He turned to find a man looming over him, regarding the check with heavy-lidded eyes.

"The amount is blank."

"I'm authorized to go as high as need be to get help," Benson said, sweating. Who was this stranger? He must have stood 6'3 and wore a suit of purple velvet under a yellow frock coat lined with thick fur.

"Your accent is charming, and your pleading makes it more so."

"I'm from Mississippi and my need is great. Give me back that check so I can hire someone who'll help me."

"Well, I'm from Ireland and *my* need is also great—for money. I don't share your fellow Americans' prejudice against paper, I assure you. My name is Oscar Wilde, I am a visitor and I will be happy to help."

Benson laughed, looking the man up and down. *"You?"*

If Benson's response annoyed him, the Irishman didn't show it. Instead he gestured at the room. No one paid them any mind, conversation and the piano music resuming just as quickly as Benson's pleadings interrupted them. "You seem to have slim options. But then I find Colorado is a place of immense thinness."

"What?"

"The air—breathless! The clouds—ribbons! The people—wraiths! The wind makes the dust dance in narrow wisps and the plants have spindles for leaves. This check is drawn on the account of a William Bruckner. Who is he?"

"My employer. I am Mr. Bruckner's gardener."

He found Wilde's eyes brightening, a strange contrast to the sorrow in his expression. "I fear for the fate of botanists in this land. But here miners are the true gardeners, aren't they? Their flowers bloom underground. Two days ago I was lowered into darkness to see a cultivation of gold blossoms, each petal glinting by oil lamp. A cold bouquet indeed."

"Mr. Bruckner might agree with you. He is a metallurgist and an engineer. Have you heard of the Bruckner Cylinder Furnace?"

"Should I have?"

"In Georgetown and beyond, the machine has brought Mr. Bruckner high esteem."

"And wealth enough to have a personal gardener in this unpromising climate."

Benson squared his shoulders, prepared to detail the pride he took in his work. Then he realized how he was falling under the Irishman's spell of complacency.

"Come with me then—if you'll truly help. I'll take *anyone* at this point."

He held out his hand for the check, but Wilde only folded it and tucked it into his breast pocket.

They were in a coach less than an hour later—merely the time it took for Wilde to have his trunk loaded. The Irishman seemed to swell to fill the space of the carriage, so that Benson felt he must draw up his knees to be accommodating. The fur lining of Wilde's frock coat settled around the back of his neck like a peacock's plumage. A cravat of purple silk was knotted and bowed at his Adam's apple and he wore his hair as long as a woman's.

"Would you be so good as to explain what trouble Georgetown is having? Since no one in Leadville seemed to care one way or the other, I didn't have the opportunity to eavesdrop."

"Leadville!" Benson said. "I only came there because they're the nearest place of any size. I should have known they wouldn't care."

GEORGETOWN HAUNTS AND MYSTERIES

"I take it there's a rivalry?"

Benson shook his head. "They mine gold there. In Georgetown it's silver."

"A schism worthy of Catholics and Protestants. But what is troubling Georgetown that you come seeking help with a blank check?"

"It began when William—"

Wilde leaned forward. "Who is William?"

"I meant Mr. Bruckner."

"Your employer."

"Yes."

"And you call him by his Christian name?"

Benson's fingers curled against his palms. "I don't know why I said that. It's not proper."

"That's what makes it so American. Please continue."

"Men came to see Mr. Bruckner. He is older and reclusive now. But they kept insisting he go with him. I know he'd given them an improved version of his furnace, and it seemed they had questions. He relented and went with them, but returned less than an hour later, badly shaken. He took straight to bed and babbled in German."

"Is that his native tongue? Was William once *Wilhelm?*"

"Yes," Benson said.

"And you don't know German?"

"Very little. Only *mein liebster freund.*"

"*My dearest friend,*" Wilde said automatically. "I had a German governess as a boy. She taught me her language, and its stories. I'm curious who taught you that phrase."

Benson's cheeks flushed. "There are many Germans in Georgetown. I overheard it."

"Eavesdropping is the thrifty man's college."

"Well, the next day, in town, I heard people talking about strange problems in the mines. One old shaft suddenly flooded full of water, drowning several men. Another miner said his bore holes ran red and wet, like the rock walls were bleeding."

"Strange occurrences indeed," Wilde said. "But surely not enough to make you flee in search of help."

Benson stared out the coach window and shivered. "When I went back to gardening, I was on my hands and knees, pulling at a weed. The root was excessively long. I pulled and pulled. Then—suddenly—something pulled back. A force yanked so hard I was thrown face down into the dirt. I swear I heard a whisper coming up through the earth, and that made me run inside."

Wilde drew his coat around him. "This is truly wonderful and unexpected. It's been a long time since we lived in an age of wonders. Instead we live in an age of marvels, which is not the same thing at all."

"What's the difference?"

"Marvels are constructed—engineered—while wonders happen naturally. Or perhaps I should say they are engineered by . . . a different power, one the mind of man at present has little consideration for. Wonders are often very small, I think, like a moment of fidelity in marriage. Marvels are always large. Mr. Bruckner's furnace strikes me as a great marvel. It conjures visions of enormity."

"It is large. A man could sit upon another man's shoulders and still not see over the central chamber."

"And what does it do?"

"Removes sulfur from ore."

"Sulfur?"

"I couldn't tell you how it's done. But with the sulfur removed, the ore becomes far more valuable. His new enhancements have increased the furnace's speed and power. The smell of sulfur is particularly strong when the cylinders stop. That means more has been extracted from the ore."

Wilde sat back, a bemused smiled on his face. He began to laugh.

"What is it?" Benson said.

"I think I've deduced the problem."

Benson leaned forward. "What is it, Wilde?"

"Quite simply, I think the Devil has come to Georgetown."

"Odd the station's so empty," Wilde said, emerging from the coach when they arrived the next day. Benson was already out and looking around, and seeing Wilde squeeze his body from the narrow confines reminded him of a caterpillar emerging from its cocoon as simply a larger caterpillar, no butterfly transformation in evidence.

"It's still in the early morning."

"If the people of Georgetown don't agree with the sunrise, I shall find myself most happy here. Dawn is best experienced at noon."

Benson walked around the coach. They were by the train station, at the edge of town, and even in the early morning one normally found people milling here and there, along with several dogs looking for a handout. He turned his gaze to the mountains whose slopes created the valley where Georgetown nestled. The fresh morning light did nothing to change his first impression from over a year ago. They were piteously ugly from aggressive logging, leaving stumps and sickly underbrush most prominent to observation.

He became aware of an unearthly silence. Normally the mountains hummed with the sound of equipment, the steam engines and oar carts that put the hillsides under siege. Even at night, when the miners turned their attention to drink and the streets echoed with rowdy intrigues, one heard above it all the massive waterwheels cranking as water from the Georgetown reservoir sluiced down through the Guanella Pass over a mile away and dropped down upon them some 700 feet.

Even *they* were silent.

Benson returned to find Wilde staring at the blank check. He scowled. "You seem incredibly unconcerned about this. Yesterday you thought we were dealing with nothing short of Satan."

"Merely a *quip*. But the Devil is rather impractical as an explanation for Georgetown's troubles. If the coachman will be so good as to take my trunk down, we'll then go and see your William—excuse me, your Mr. Bruckner."

59

Benson turned to the coach. The driver wasn't there. He regarded Wilde, who'd noticed the absence too. "He must have gone inside the station manager's office," Benson said, and went over to see. The door was locked. He peered inside the dusty window.

Empty.

He returned to Wilde with his hands up and open. The Irishman laughed. "Our coach was driverless? Perhaps the Devil deserves more credence."

"We must find Mr. Bruckner right away," Benson said, pivoting to head into town. But Wilde grabbed his shoulder.

"My trunk," he said.

"You can't be serious."

"Not usually, but I'm afraid I insist on my luggage. And as you're the only manual laborer in an area where things seem to disappear rather quickly, I'd like my trunk removed before the carriage itself becomes. . . immaterial."

Benson cursed in disbelief, but he climbed up and unstrapped the box, lugging it down with a thud. "Here are your damn clothes!"

Wilde bent to unlatch the lid. "It's the accessories that make the outfit." Benson watched him sift through layer upon layer of fabric until, after a minute of digging, Wilde held up a silver pistol for the sunlight's worship.

"That's beautiful," Benson said.

"A Webley Bull Dog. At the moment, the United Kingdom's second most popular export to America—after myself. I received it as a gift in Leadville the day before meeting you. Funny how the best souvenirs of home are those you travel thousands of miles to obtain. Nevertheless, it's fully loaded and I believe in excellent working order. The Devil, dear Benson, doesn't stand a chance."

⁂

They had only taken a few steps toward town when the station manager's door opened and a horribly aged dwarf stepped out, shrunken and stooped, his shoulders dominated by a hump. The air turned solid in Benson's lungs as he saw the man's shriveled face. A decrepit, clawed finger rose in caution against grinning lips.

This was not a human being.

"Fire, Wilde," Benson managed.

The Irishman raised the gun but didn't shoot.

"Finde mich—finde sie—wo meine Blumen wachsen."

The thing laughed and raised its hands. The earth trembled at once, throwing Benson and Wilde off their feet. A sinkhole opened up beneath the creature's feet and it slipped out of sight as surely as a ship caught in a whirlpool. Wilde scrambled up, pulling Benson with him and they stared down a perfectly round chasm no wider than a person.

"How far down do you think it goes?"

"Deeper than even the bravest Alice would dare."

"That *thing* spoke to us."

"In German—curiously enough."

"What did it say, Wilde?"

"The creature told us to find it—and *them*—in the place where its flowers grow. It seems you're not the only cultivator in the area, Benson. Though I fear for the lover who receives a bouquet from *its* garden."

"Let's find Mr. Bruckner."

"Indeed," Wilde said. "Let's find *anyone*."

The streets were as empty as the station. Benson rushed up to the door of D.H. Miller's barbershop and barged through. All he found were quantities of hair all over the floor. A queer sensation overtook Benson. He imagined several people simply vanishing out from underneath their scalps, leaving the hair to fall like tufts of feathers in their wake.

Wilde waited for him outside. "I tried the office of your town newspaper. There were no reporters, no editors, not even a telegraph operator."

"This can't be," Benson said. "Where did everyone go? Ten thousand people live here!"

They reached the McClellan Opera House on the corner of 6th and Taos. A placard outside read—

One Night Only
Callender's Minstrels!
A Collossol Congress of Colored Celebrities!
Beautiful Scenery
Life-Like Pictures
Old-Time Songs
The Steamboat Race
The Levee Roustabouts

"One night? This sign looks more weathered than that."

"It went up just before I left for Leadville."

"Then the town must have emptied very quickly thereafter."

Benson reared back and kicked the placard onto its side and stomped it.

"Appropriately theatrical," Wilde said.

A slow, squealing sound drew their attention. The opera house door opened, and three more creatures like the dwarf from the station office stepped out. They looked identical and carried pickaxes. The trio gave a disagreeable sneer and twisted away from the sunlight.

Wilde grabbed Benson's elbow. "They're blinded— seize our chance." They started running with the quietest footfalls they could manage, a tiptoed dash up the block to the corner of the bank. Benson pressed his back flat to the brick and panted. After a year in Georgetown, he thought he'd gotten used to the thin air. Panic had reverted him back to his first day.

Wilde risked a glance. "I see them. They're going in the opposite direction."

Benson looked too and thought back to his childhood. After the war, when he was only five, Union troops were stationed in his town and they made regular harassing patrols in the streets, knocking on doors at all hours of the day and night. They made his mother cry. Remembering her tears, Benson's loathing rose. The creatures moved from building to building, dragging the heads of their pickaxes behind them, generating small clouds of dirt in their wake.

There was a scream.

"My God," Benson said as a boy came running from one of the buildings. The creatures raised their pickaxes and pursued. Their gait reminded Benson of a goose, but their swiftness was more like geese in flight. They fell upon the boy. Benson felt a burst of heat from Wilde's body and saw his right hand gripping the Webley very tight.

The creatures stepped away, revealing heavy manacles on the child's wrists and ankles. A metal collar seemed to weigh the boy's neck down.

"How?" Benson said.

"It's as if they forged them from the dirt."

They watched one monster pull the boy on the end of a chain. The other two continued their patrol.

"Where are they taking him?"

Wilde did not respond right away. Then, softly, he said, "The mines. And I wager that's where the rest of the populace is, too. Which mine is largest?"

"I have no idea. There must be hundreds of different shafts. Maybe thousands."

"Surely you have some idea of which—"

"I'm a gardener! Don't act like I'm supposed to *know* anything about the mines."

"Of course not," Wilde said, holding out his hands in a placating gesture. "I only wish I'd paid more attention when I made my descent in Leadville. My guides were eager to explain the process and procedures of mining, but I was too enthralled with the poetry of their bodies to care much about the prose of their labor."

Benson clamped his teeth down against a gasp at such frankness. Wilde flashed amusement but graveness soon returned, and Benson stepped back as the Irishman straightened to his full height. His hair was damp and the beads of sweat on his forehead looked unnatural. Sweat belonged on Wilde's broad white brow about as much as sea foam should be found on a cactus.

"I've been puzzling over why the creature should speak in German. It makes me wonder about something, Benson. I said sulfur was the Devil's odor, and that's so. But perhaps it's the scent of other monstrosities as well."

"I don't understand."

"I'm not sure there is anything to understand yet. How far away is Mr. Bruckner's house?"

"Five blocks."

"Then we must hurry. He might be there if he is as reclusive as you say. These patrols are either poorly sighted or not very thorough if a boy could have eluded them this long. They might not expend the energy on a solitary old man."

They again broke into a pace of quick but careful steps that nevertheless rang like alarm bells in Benson's mind. He imagined his tread sending tremors into the earth, identifying their location. Any moment the earth would open up in a personal sinkhole to hell.

They reached the house and stood in astonishment.

"You, sir, *are* a most remarkable gardener."

In any other circumstance, Benson would have cherished the remark. Instead the words chilled him by confirming his eyes weren't playing tricks. The front yard blazed with blooms of yellow, purple, red and blue. The clusters grew so thick it was as if the yard had been seeded with flowers rather than grass.

"This . . . this is not my doing."

"Are you sure?"

"I think I'd know! My own garden is my own garden," Benson said. "I don't even recognize these plants. Most of my focus was on asters. They seemed to do the best for the soil and climate. But they shouldn't be blooming until months from now."

"I have a small knowledge of flowers, Benson. These *aren't* asters."

"No."

He bent to touch one. Wilde told him to stop, but he ignored the caution. He pinched one golden bloom and received such confusion from his fingertips he jerked his hand away.

"What is it, Benson?"

"It's cold—*icy*. And the texture . . ."

"Go on."

"The petals felt hard—like metal."

He heard a distinct cry from the upstairs window. Benson's attention riveted upon the front door. "William," he said automatically, and raced onto the porch. Wilde caught him.

"We must be cautious!"

"To hell with caution. William screamed—"

"Or someone impersonated his scream. But we are past such cautions now. The cry came from upstairs. The bedroom, I take it?"

66

"I know nothing about Mr. Bruckner's bedroom."

"Do you not sleep here as well?"

"I'm Mr. Bruckner's *gardener.*"

"Then one wonders at the strange alchemy turning *Mr. Bruckner* into *William* and back again so rapidly in your thoughts."

"You *dare—*"

"Yes, Benson, I dare *many* things. Let Socrates huff away about the unexamined life. Since the invention of neighbors and newspapers, such examinations are easy to come by. But the *unchallenged* life is solely one's own fault—and the true impetus for all my actions."

He took out the blank check, tore it in half and let the separate pieces fall on the ground.

"We must have honesty or our endeavors here will fail. Come—lead me upstairs either to *your* bedroom or to *Mr. Bruckner's*—for I know they are one in the same."

Benson trembled, his heartbeat now so fast it seemed undetectable in his chest. He led Wilde into the house and up the steps. The bedroom door was closed and Wilde drew his Webley.

"Bruckner?" he called.

William's voice answered, feverish and rambling snippets of German he did not comprehend until suddenly—clearly—he perceived a key phrase:

"*—mein liebster freund—*"

He turned the knob, found it locked, and threw his shoulder against the door. Wilde joined him. The heavy wood shook as its frame creaked and splintered. Then it gave way and they stumbled through.

Two figures rested on the bed, apparently oblivious to the assault on the door. One was William—or some approximation of him. Benson's attention focused on the second. Something decrepit clutched William to its bosom. Grinning, gloating, a living sickness caressed William's left cheek with clawed fingers and drew the feverish sweat of his brow to taste in a lipless mouth.

William tried to sound out a word, but made only the same stutter—"*Koh—koh—koh—*"

"Kobold," Wilde said, and as if his voice gave the first indication of their presence, the nasty creature that cradled William snarled as it rose to a stature no less terrifying for its unimpressive height. In the confines of the room, the creature's body odor became stifling, a stench of crushed earthworms in loose, wet, stagnant soil. Its mottled skin reminded Benson of how his hands looked after digging in the garden, the natural paleness stained dark with heavier motes of dirt clinging in his hair like little moles and blisters.

"Kobold," Wilde repeated, stepping forward with the Webley raised. "My suspicions are confirmed. I know exactly what your kind is now."

He shot, and the creature sprang up, taking up a pick-axe Benson had not noticed. In a blur it swung the head around and Wilde's bullet deflected off it in a cascade of white sparks. The brief flare made the creature grimace and gave Benson his best look at William's face.

Only half of it remained human.

My God, what has the thing done to him?

Wilde kept the Webley trained on the monster. "Shall we duel, Kobold—the wonder of your magic versus the marvel of my gun?"

The thing leapt to the challenge. Wilde fired. If the gun hit the creature, the bullet had no effect. Benson dove as the pickaxe swung, narrowly missing his face. He looked up just as Wilde shot point blank into the fiend's head. The impact sent it staggering against the foot of the bed. There it slumped. Benson experienced a moment of exultation—the thing was *dead*. But reality would not be denied. The creature reached up and pulled the bullet from the wound, holding it up before its eyes. "Köstliches silber."

It popped the bullet into its mouth like a date and chewed.

"My earlier assessment is confirmed, Benson," Wilde said, backing off fast. "Wonders are much superior to marvels."

The creature held its pickaxe up and followed. Wilde raised his hands in a last ditch effort at self-defense as the axe swung at him.

"Hör auf damit!"

William's voice. Benson saw him on his knees, reaching out toward the monster, which had frozen its attack. He went on speaking in German and the foul, misshapen dwarf answered back. Then it grabbed Wilde's right arm and began to drag him.

Wilde shouted and beat against his captor to no avail. Benson moved to help but William squeezed his shoulder with his transformed right hand. The claw-like fingers dug into his muscle.

69

"He's beyond your reach, Ben."

"He's here to help us!"

"Why are you here? I told you to run. I gave you the check to draw upon all my assets."

"I gave your check to *him*. I just wanted to get back here."

The remaining human half of William's face showed despair. "One person? Even an army won't help Georgetown now."

"What's happening? What was it Wilde said?"

"Kobold."

"That creature knew it."

"It reacted to its name. Kobold is *all* of their names. And it's *my* name."

Benson shook his head. "You're human, no matter what that thing was trying to do to you."

"It wasn't trying to make me wear a mask, Ben. It was trying to rip off the one I've been wearing."

"William, no—"

"I can't expect you to understand. I'm—the last of my kind. Or so I thought. How can I even attempt an explanation? I woke in darkness. I lived in darkness. There were none like me. When I hungered, I chewed rock and ore and was content—but so alone."

"William, you've lived in Georgetown more than twenty years. You're an engineer. You came here from Germany—"

He laughed bitterly. "Deep below it."

Benson's thoughts became a chaos. William worked his way out from under the blanket and sheet, revealing how his transformation extended further down his body. The sight provoked a sharp inhale from Benson, who turned his face to the wall.

"I'll never believe you're one of *them*."

"I deserve your rebuke and your hatred. What's happened is my fault. I did not realize the consequences of my actions."

William got out of bed. His right leg had shriveled up to a stumpy length, essentially leaving him an amputee. He balanced on his left foot, left hand bracing him against the wall. Benson saw this in his peripheral vision and William's struggle goaded him into standing too.

"What *are* your actions? How can you be responsible?"

"I encountered my first human in 1845—a young man adventuring on his own. I did not realize then that I lived deep inside a mine that had been abandoned many years. This man had become lost, and I heard his terror and came to investigate. When I stepped into the light of his lantern, he shouted, 'Kobold!' and fled. Not understanding, I gave chase and captured him. He told me what I was. A creature of the dark, a spirit of the mines. I kept him with me despite his pleas, not understanding how his needs differed from mine until he died. Then I knew sorrow—and loss—and bitterness. Above all I had understanding and vowed to quit the darkness. I found I could take his shape, and I walked into the sunlight in his clothes. I have lived the life he might have lived. But the mines pulled at my heart. I had to be near them. I put an ocean between myself and my origins and came here, to this place where the humans seemed so very much like me in their core. I tried to help them. I made my furnace—and it was my undoing."

"The smell of sulfur."

"Yes. Horrible to you. But to me it was like the scent of myself, the whiff of memory. And I knew there was something about the ore these men mined. Some *trace* of my own being—my own people. For many years I fought the urge to investigate. And then I met you."

Benson's lower lip trembled. "What could I have to do with any of this?"

"You gave me love. I thought I could give it back—"

"You did!"

"No, Ben. I tried. But—I was always lonely, and it grew worse in your company. This is not your fault. In a fashion, you and I have both been in a search for our own kind. Your strength convinced me to indulge a suspicion that more like me existed, but incorporeal and trapped within the rocks themselves. I altered my furnace in an attempt to bring them forth physically. And so I have—to this world's peril."

"How many are there?"

"Seven. More than enough to subjugate Georgetown."

"Seven against ten thousand!"

"You saw the effects of your friend's gun. The bullet is meaningless. But these kobolds are not the same as me. They are vengeful and malignant. I tried to plead with them but they wouldn't listen. They say there are thousands more of them awaiting their freedom, and only my furnace can do it. They don't know how to operate it though. That's the only reason my defiance hasn't brought death. They must be stopped."

"But how, if even guns won't work?"

"Help me downstairs. Help me—into the garden."

"The flowers," William said, pointing to the deceptive blooms of cold metal. "Those are your weapons."

"How am I supposed to kill your people with *flowers,* no matter how strange they are?"

"They're not mere flowers, as you've already guessed. I forged them from the earth with the help of a power the kobolds don't comprehend—the power of your intention. You have thought your labors pointless and futile, but every bead of sweat you let fall into the soil was a seed of hope, and that hope carries into the blooms. Wield them as a dagger is wielded. Drive the petals into their backs."

Hesitating a moment, Benson knelt and gingerly pulled at a stem. It came free of the soil with a metallic sound, like a sword exiting a scabbard. The flower had almost no heft to it and yet he sensed tremendous power in the blooms.

"Quickly now. Gather your bouquet. Seven at least. No—eight. There must be eight."

"Why eight if there are seven of them?"

William stared at Benson until he understood.

"No," Benson said.

"You must, Ben. I'm not sure I know myself. I'm not sure this remorse I feel will last. I hear the mines calling to me more than ever. I hear the song of my people, and

73

even if I am against them now, they *are* my kind. Take the eighth bloom. *There.* Now put it in the vase of my heart."

The ground began to tremble.

"Hurry, Ben! They're coming for us!"

He stepped forward. As he did, a sinkhole appeared on the spot he'd just occupied. He lunged forward into the embrace of William's human arm. It wrapped around his waist. His clawed hand took Benson's wrist and raised the flower to his chest.

More sinkholes appeared. The house itself shook, the roof starting to buckle.

"Now, Ben!"

Crying, he drove the stem against William's chest, still convinced it would simply bend and break. But William's mouth opened in a silent scream, and blood that was not red poured forth.

Then the sky sank out of sight.

He picked himself up and clutched the bouquet, as the sound of people crying grew louder. Benson scarcely believed the scene in front of him. A subterranean kingdom was being constructed, and the men, women, and children of Georgetown labored in chains to expand its borders. They had no tools other than their fingernails.

A kobold stood glaring at him, its pickaxe raised. The creature charged him, swinging his weapon as he went. Benson drew a yellow flower and held it out, unable to help feeling foolish.

Until the bloom began to glow.

It flashed like the sun, and the kobold groaned and stopped, squeezing its eyes closed. Benson shot forward and plunged the bloom against the kobold's throat. At once the thing howled and the bloom burst into flames. The kobold pulled back, taking the flower out of Benson's grip. He watched the monster tugging on the stem but the flower only sank deeper into its throat.

The kobold fell forward onto its face and lay motionless.

"Benson!"

He spun and found Wilde at the entrance to a new shaft, laboring under heavy chains. Several cuts marked his face. He looked so worn and beaten Benson could not believe he'd been enslaved less than thirty minutes ago.

"I feel like I've been digging for days," he said, holding up his fingers. Wilde's nails were splintered and dark. "I think time must be experienced differently in the dominion of the kobold."

"How did you know their name?" Benson said as he tried to break the shackles.

"As I said, my German governess taught me both her language and its stories, particularly fairytales. And as I've learned in my travels in these states and territories, *everything* has an American cousin. Can you free me?"

Benson regarded the bouquet. He separated one flower from the rest and touched it against Wilde's collar. The invincible iron turned to dirt and Wilde's eyes gleamed. His wrists and ankles were freed in minutes.

"If civilization survives the kobolds, I'll have to add a segment to my lecture tour about the power of flowers. May I?"

He took three stems and held them up for inspection. "A wonder *and* a marvel. Let's get to work, Benson. The war of the roses demands a sequel!"

When it was done, they led the people of Georgetown out of the mines and into the light. From their condition and reaction, Benson figured Wilde's assessment was right: Time must have moved differently in the mines. The men looked grizzled, their hair exceedingly long and filthy. Boys and girls no longer fit into their clothes. Everyone staggered as if not encountering sunlight in a year.

But they were alive.

Wilde said as much as the two of them trekked back to the ruins of William's house. When they arrived, they found the wondrous flowers were gone. There was only William, dead, his human disguise entirely ended.

"It's a shame you must remember him like this."

"I remember the person I loved. Nothing else matters. But no one else must know his identity."

"I shall be happy to help you bury someone so noble."

"No," Benson said, wiping his eyes before bending to take the small body into his arms. "I will do this alone."

He went off to sow a final seed as Mr. Bruckner's gardener.

SEAN EADS

Sean Eads is a writer and librarian living in Denver, Colorado. His second novel, *The Survivors*, was a finalist for the 2013 Lambda Literary Award. His latest novel, *Lord Byron's Prophecy*, was a finalist for the Colorado Book Award and the Shirley Jackson Award.

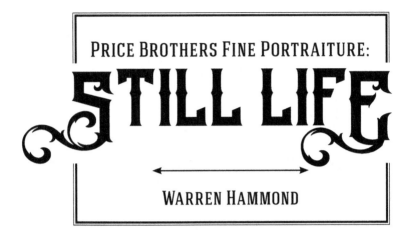

PRICE BROTHERS FINE PORTRAITURE:
STILL LIFE

WARREN HAMMOND

APRIL, 1883

Agatha Price had never touched anything so cold as the hand of her younger sister. Its icy touch leaked through the thick fabric of her dress. She shivered at the thought of it, but it was more than a thought. That hand was actually resting on her right knee, weeping with the same kind of cold that crept through the crack between door and jamb.

Much as she wanted to brush the still hand off her knee, she knew she couldn't without detaching the pins and lasso of thin thread holding it lifelessly in place. Seated side by side on a velvet settee, Agatha sensed her sister starting to tip, and quickly reached over Jane's shoulder to pull her back into an awkward recline. Even the embalming couldn't hide the whiff of rot that made Agatha wince.

Her eyes began to sting, but not from the odor. Jane was only a year younger than Agatha's fifteen, and Agatha couldn't remember a time when they weren't inseparable. Attached at the hip her father used to say.

Jane's head lolled forward, and Agatha pushed it gently back into position. "Really, Father, how much longer before we get this portrait completed?"

From a seat next to the wood stove on the far side of the portraiture studio, Orville Price let out a long sigh that had become more and more of a habit since Jane took ill. "Let's give your mother another minute, Agatha."

"Where's Uncle Thad?"

"He just went around the corner to settle our dining tab at the Hotel de Paris. He'll be right back."

Agatha nodded, hoping he returned quickly. It seemed like Uncle Thadeaus was the only person left who could perk her father up and make him laugh like he used to. Most of the time, he sulked about the house.

As did her mother.

As did she.

For months, she'd limited her sulking to late at night or during Jane's long daytime sleeps. The rest of the time, Agatha was too busy playing nurse, bringing food three times daily, and twice daily, haranguing her sister into getting out of bed for her doctor-prescribed regimen of exercises. She patted her sister's back when she coughed, and she constantly worked to keep the sink and bedding clean of phlegm and blood.

Her mother helped too, of course, but despite the protestations of her parents, it was Agatha who did the most. The sisters always were inseparable. Even now, it was Agatha who held her sister up, a hand tucked under Jane's arm, which had been withered thin as dry tinder by her months-long fight against the consumption.

The door opened, and Agatha braced herself against the icy blast ushering Uncle Thad inside. Quickly, he lashed the door before turning around. He was a full eight years younger than Agatha's father, still a young man by anybody's standard. Seeing Agatha and Jane together on the settee, he removed the bowler from his head and offered a considerate nod.

Like her father, Uncle Thad was dressed in black. The trousers and vest were part of his normal wardrobe, but the waistcoat was a loaner from the rack of finery standing against the wall. It had taken two years to gather that donning collection for their less well-to-do customers, two years since the success of the silver mines brought the family from Baltimore to Georgetown carrying little more than the camera her father used to found *Price's Fine Portraiture*. It wasn't until a year later, the studio established, that Uncle Thad crossed the Great Plains to join the photography business, and the sign was repainted to say *Price Brothers Fine Portraiture*.

"Your father asked me to get something for you," said Uncle Thad.

"For me?" asked Agatha. She looked at her father. "So all this waiting has been a ruse?"

He tipped his head, but couldn't manage a smile.

Uncle Thad stepped forward and reached into his waistcoat to pull out a silver locket and chain. Agatha propped her sister up and used her hip to wedge Jane in place before letting go with her hands to reach for the locket. "It's beautiful."

"There's a hasp on the side."

Agatha used a fingernail to pry it open. The name *Jane* was engraved on the inside. "It's perfect, Uncle Thad."

"We'll take a curl of her hair and store it in the locket so she'll always be close."

Agatha's father, who was now standing alongside his brother, asked, "You bought one for Hortense too?"

"I most certainly did, Orville."

The brothers embraced, and for the first time since Jane started to cough, Agatha felt like it all might be okay.

"Did I hear my name?" Agatha's mother called from the top of the stairs. She came down, careful to lift the hem of her black dress. Her red hair had been parted down the center and pulled back to be concealed under a black scarf. Uncle Thad pulled an identical locket out of his coat pocket and let it swing from its chain, a broad smile fighting for space under a bushy moustache.

Hortense Price turned around and lifted her scarf to expose the back of her neck. Taking the locket from his brother, Orville lifted the chain over his wife's head and hooked the clasp. Staying seated, Agatha pulled her brown curls to the side so her uncle could do the same for her.

Uncle Thad stood back to admire the locket. "That's going to make for a beautiful picture. Maybe I should've gotten one for Jane too?"

"Nonsense," said Hortense. "This portrait will be perfect as is."

"Very well," said Uncle Thad before heading into the black room. "I'll get the plate ready."

Agatha's mother patted the locket hanging on her chest and looked at Jane. "Oh, Agatha, you've done a splendid job with those ringlets. They were her favorite."

Agatha's heart swelled with pride. She and her sister had been dressing each other's hair since they were old enough to hold a brush.

Her parents took positions behind the settee, and each of them rested a hand upon one of their daughter's shoulders. When Agatha felt the squeeze of her father's fingers, she leaned her head back and smiled up at him. Yes, she'd miss Jane every single day of her life, but it was all going to be okay.

Uncle Thad returned with the tintype plate encased in its holder and slid the holder into position at the back of the camera. Ducking under the curtain, he slightly adjusted the camera angle before stepping around the tripod to the front.

He looked his brother's family over to make sure everything was perfect, and then he removed the lens cap. Agatha counted to eight in her head as she tried to hold still. She'd seen her father and uncle do dozens of remembrance portraits like this one, and she always found it eerie that, because the departed were much better at keeping still for the lens's long exposure, the deceased's image came out sharper than the living.

Uncle Thad put the cap back in place. "Let's see how this one comes out." He pulled the plate holder from the back of the camera, and Agatha's father went to join him in the black room.

The process would only take a few minutes, and Agatha and her mother passed the time discussing plans for their trip back to Baltimore to bury Jane amongst family. They hadn't been back in two years, and her mother was looking forward to seeing her brothers. They'd depart, the three of them, as soon as this springtime cold snap passed. Uncle Thad could run the business until they returned in summer.

Finally, her father entered the room. Without masking his annoyance, he wordlessly stepped back into position behind her. Uncle Thad came in next, another tintype in hand, a sheepish smile on his face. "I erred on that one," he said. "Took the cloth off the window too early."

Uncle Thad repeated the process of preparing the camera. "Ready?" he asked, his hand on the lens cap.

Agatha nodded. The lens cap was removed, and she spent the eight-count wondering why her father's grip on her shoulder was so tight. The exposure complete, the Price Brothers again closed themselves inside the black room.

Agatha fussed in her seat. One of the pins holding the thread looped about her sister's wrist had begun to poke.

"I know you're uncomfortable," said her mother. "But I'm sure this plate will be perfect. When was the last time you saw either of them make a mistake two times in a row?"

Jane began to slip forward again, but this time it was her mother who pulled her back into position. The door opened, and the Price brothers marched through. Right away, Agatha knew something was amiss. She could see it in the tightness of shoulders and jaws.

"What's wrong?" asked Agatha.

Neither her father nor uncle met her gaze. "We have to do it again," was all her father said when his hand dropped heavily upon her shoulder.

Agatha worked to control her racing thoughts as she held still for another eight-second exposure. Had she done something wrong?

Before she could ask, the brothers headed for the black room again, but this time her mother decided to follow. She stopped at the door to look back at Agatha. "Once again, it appears they need a woman's help," she said trying her best to offer a casual smile. But she failed. Agatha could see the concern in her mother's eyes.

The door closed, leaving Agatha alone with her sister. The cold hand still resting unnaturally upon her knee.

She felt her heart beating inside her chest. Her pulse rapped at her temples. But why was she suddenly so anxious? The actions of the adults around her were indeed disconcerting, but in the end, it was just a photograph. What could be so horrible?

She felt hot, almost like a fever had taken hold. Thankfully, the wind picked up outside, and a draft from the window blew on her shoulders. She luxuriated in the chill, thinking this must be one of those astonishingly frigid winds that creeped across the ice and snowcapped

Continental Divide before tumbling downhill, gathering speed like an avalanche until it barreled into Georgetown.

The adults reentered the room, their postures tense, their lips sealed, and again, Agatha sat through the eight-second ritual while her father's fingernails dug into her collar bone.

"What's the problem?" she asked.

But no response came before her father and uncle again disappeared into the black room. This time her mother went to the kitchen instead. To start a pot of coffee she said.

Alone again, she decided she'd had quite enough of being ignored. So Agatha pulled the pins attached to her dress and let her sister's hand and the thread wrapped about Jane's wrist slip from her knee. Taking care to lay her sister on the settee, she went to the black room door and pressed her ear against the wood. Inside, she heard the clacking sounds of jars and the metal-on-metal scrape of the water pump. She waited long enough to be sure the image was light-safe before turning the doorknob slow and quiet. She pushed the door slowly open.

The cloth had already been pulled from the window, and her father and uncle faced the workbench. Up on the wall, a row of three fully developed tintypes stood side-by-side on a shelf. The fourth and most recent plate stood inside a bell jar on the workbench taking a developer bath.

Agatha stepped forward, the floorboards creaking under her feet. Her father and uncle didn't turn toward the noise, probably assuming it was her mother who had entered the room.

The photos all possessed excellent quality. Puzzled, she wondered why the adults in her family had been so aflutter. To her eye, the photos would all make fantastic memento mori.

Her father bent close to look inside the jar, his voice barely audible. "It's just like the others."

Then she saw it. A gasp escaped from her throat.

Her father turned around. He stepped up to her and took her hands in his. He leaned down to match her eye-to-eye, his voice colored by desperation. "It doesn't mean anything, Agatha. It's just a trick of the camera. We see strange things all the time, isn't that right, Thad?"

"It sure is," said Uncle Thad, his face pale behind that thick moustache. "The camera often picks up oddities."

Agatha looked over her father's shoulder. What she saw was no oddity or random distortion. All four portraits were exactly the same. All showed the slightly fuzzy images of her mother and father when compared to the perfectly sharp likeness of Jane.

She studied herself in the photos. In each and every one, her image was crystal clear.

Nobody could possibly hold that still for eight long seconds, yet the lines of her face were perfectly etched just like those of the settee and the rug and all of the other inanimate objects.

Including Jane. Who had passed from this world.

Agatha heard a wail from her mother in the kitchen. Her mother knew what the photos meant, and so did her father, tears welling in his eyes. "Please, Agatha, it's just a trick. Nothing bad is going to happen to you. We'll give it an hour, and we'll take the picture again, and you'll see it will be different."

"I feel dizzy," said Agatha. She pulled a hand from her father's grasp to raise it to her mouth, and she coughed. It was a deep wracking cough that made her entire chest feel like she'd breathed in a wasp. She held out her hand, her palm and fingers speckled with blood.

Her father opened his mouth to speak, but no words came forth. What could he say? The simple truth was Agatha's time would be short and dark with suffering.

Agatha's eyes were fixed on her sister, lying prone on the settee.

"We always were inseparable," she said.

❧

WARREN HAMMOND

Warren Hammond is a Denver-based author known for his gritty, futuristic *KOP* series. By taking the best of classic detective noir, and reinventing it on a destitute colony world, Warren has created these uniquely dark tales of murder, corruption and redemption. *KOP Killer* won the 2012 Colorado Book Award for best mystery. Warren's latest novel, *Tides of Maritinia*, released in December of 2014. His first book independent of the *KOP* series, *Tides* is a spy novel set in a science fiction-al world. Always eager to see new places, Warren has traveled extensively. Whether it's wildlife viewing in exotic locales like Botswana and the Galapagos Islands, or trekking in the Himalayas, he's always up for a new adventure.

87

PRICE BROTHERS FINE PORTRAITURE:

AFTERLIFE

ANGIE HODAPP

OCTOBER, 1885

Enoch Temberly and his young bride, Amelia, arrived in Georgetown on a cold day in October 1885. They arrived by train and, despite the pall of an early winter biting at the mountain air, set up a black-and-white-striped tent at the center of town. The sign outside the tent read, in a heavily ornamented script, "TEMBERLY'S TRAVELING MUSEUM OF THE MACABRE. GHASTLY CURIOS! ABERRANT ARTIFACTS! SUPERNATURAL RELICS! THREE DAYS ONLY! ADMISSION TEN CENTS."

For two days, nearly everyone in Georgetown—the miners, the businessmen, even the priggish school-marm—lined up to drop coins into Amelia Temberly's delicate, outstretched hand. Rumor had it the minister from Grace Episcopal went twice.

By the third day, the only Georgetown resident not to purchase admission was Thaddeus Price.

From the front window of Price Brothers Fine Portraiture, Thad watched the autumnal wind whip the corners of the tent and twist Amelia's aubergine skirts about her slender ankles. He watched the endless queue of giddy patrons file in one end of the tent and out the other. He watched Enoch himself, tall and thin and something like a spider in his black suit and stovepipe hat, help a pale-faced woman, swooning and no doubt overcome by the sight of some ghastly curio and in sudden need of fresh air, toward a nearby park bench.

It wasn't disinterest that kept Thad away. It was his own brief acquaintance with the supernatural and his resulting belief that one should not lift the veil between the living and the dead. Not even for a peek.

When night fell on the traveling museum's third and final day in Georgetown, Thad watched Enoch escort the lovely Amelia toward the Hotel de Paris, leaving the disassembly of the tent and the packing of artifacts into dozens of steamer trunks to a trio of young men obviously in his employ. Within an hour, the site where the tent stood was vacant.

Relieved, Thad pulled the curtain over his studio's front window and locked the door. He would go upstairs to his rooms, read the latest issue of the *Rocky Mountain News* over a hot cup of tea, and retire to his bed. Not one customer crossed his threshold since the Temberlys arrived; sitting for a portrait was a mundane proposition compared to the thrilling distraction of a traveling museum. But once that spidery man and his pretty wife boarded the morning train, business would resume.

Thad patted his camera as one might pat the head of a beloved hound and turned down the lamps. But no sooner had he set his foot on the bottom stair than the door opened behind him.

He whirled about. Had he not just locked the door? Perhaps he failed to fully catch the latch.

Cold, gray twilight bled into the darkened room. There, framed in his open doorway, stood the unmistakable silhouette of Amelia Temberly.

Thad's heart thundered, and not entirely from fright. He was a young man still, one yet to encounter the familiar touch of a lover or wife, and the willowy curve of Amelia's corseted waist, accentuated by the generous swells of hip and breast, stole his breath.

"Mrs. Temberly," he said, doing his best to steady his voice. "My apologies, but I've closed for the night."

"I wonder if you might reconsider." Her voice was quiet, yet her tone conveyed a certain authority that assured Thad she would not be turned out.

He felt along the mantelpiece for a match and lit the nearest lamp. In its sallow glow, he saw the details of a beauty he had, until now, regarded only from a distance: honey-colored curls pinned up beneath a fascinator of black plumes and violet lilies, a heart-shaped face, large blue eyes fringed by dark lashes.

She seemed to regard him too, and for a moment, they simply stood in silence as though growing accustomed to each other's presence.

At last, she stepped inside and gently closed the door behind her. Her gaze rested briefly on his camera, standing sentinel in the corner of the room. "You didn't come to see our museum, Mr. Price."

For a fleeting instant, Thad smelled the funereal scent of dying roses. He narrowed his eyes and inhaled, but the scent was gone. "I don't mean to be rude, Mrs. Temberly, but how do you know me, and what do you have on display that you should care whether I see?"

"Please, call me Amelia," she said. "How could we have failed to tempt you with a shrunken head from the Amazon rainforest? A Zulu throwing spear? The skull of a three-horned goat, or the severed paw of a Himalayan snow beast?" She tilted her head and examined him as though he were a child in a candy shop and she were guessing at his favorite sweet. "Siamese twins preserved in a jar? A snake with two heads? Or maybe the rope that hanged Wild Bill Longley? The glass eye worn by a voodoo priestess adept at raising the dead?"

"I'm certain you're quite good at drumming up business, but save your breath. You've not a single thing I care to see."

She smiled, revealing a straight row of perfect, white teeth. "I'll choose not to be offended by your frankness, Mr. Price."

"Thaddeus."

She bowed her head. "Thaddeus."

He shivered at the sound of his name on her lips. "What do you want from me?"

Her smile dimmed, and once more her gaze shifted to his camera. "You have something of interest to my husband. Something he'd like very much to add to his collection."

Thad had already guessed the reason for Amelia's visit, of course, and he didn't care to waste time pretending otherwise. The camera had once proven it was capable of a certain clairvoyance. Yet in the two years since its lens had presaged the death of his beloved niece, Agatha, it had not offered a repeat performance. Every portrait Thad had taken with it since Agatha's premonitory *memento mori* had come out quite normally. Whether the camera was truly possessed of some otherworldly force, he could not fathom.

He laid a hand on the camera's wood-and-leather casing. "Did your husband send you to charm it from my keeping?"

"Quite the contrary, I assure you."

At last, she had engaged his curiosity. Amelia was undoubtedly a clever woman—she must have guessed he had no intent to let go of the device. So what could she want? And what harm in hearing her out?

He swept a hand toward the settee in the corner of the studio, a piece he often incorporated when arranging a large family or rabble of siblings. The very piece, in fact, on which both Jane and Agatha had posed for their final portrait.

The stiff fabric of Amelia's skirts whispered and shushed as she moved toward the settee. She lowered herself onto the scarlet cushion and folded her hands in her lap. "I came to warn you, Thaddeus. Enoch is accustomed to having his every desire indulged. He came to Georgetown to acquire your camera, and he'll do so, no matter the means."

Anger twisted like a thorny vine in Thad's chest. He'd be damned if that arachnid of a man stole his camera! He drew a deep breath to calm himself. "Where is your husband now?"

"At the Hotel de Paris, hosting a séance. He'll be occupied until well after midnight."

"Does he know you're here?"

She lowered her gaze. "Of course not. He thinks I've retired to my suite for the evening."

The vine in Thad's chest relaxed its barbed coils, allowing his thoughts to uncoil as well. He pulled the chair from behind his desk and positioned it so that he could sit across from her. Joining her on the settee seemed improper. "I can think of only one way Mr. Temberly came to know about the camera," he said. "You've visited Baltimore, I presume."

She nodded. "In June. Orville was one of our first visitors."

Thad stiffened at her mention of his brother. Orville had gone utterly mad with grief over the loss of his two daughters to consumption. He and his wife, Hortense, took their girls' bodies back east to be buried in the family plot. Orville left Price Brothers Fine Portraiture in Thad's charge, claiming he'd return after the girls' funerals. But Hortense fell ill, too, and died at the end of May. That left Orville standing over three fresh graves, quite alone and quite undone.

Thad had long since stopped expecting Orville to return to Georgetown. Yet he couldn't bring himself to remove the word "Brothers" from their sign.

Amelia was watching him now, silent. He gestured for her to continue.

"Orville came the second day as well. His fascination with our collection consumed him. He was obsessed. On the third day, he returned yet again and told Enoch that he, too, had once been in possession of a supernatural object—a camera that had predicted the death of his daughter." She bit her lip. "He showed us the photographs you took of Jane and Agatha."

Thad clenched his jaw. How well he remembered that dreadful day. Permeating the air, lying just beneath the thick, chemical odor of embalming fluid, lay the stench of death. He and Orville posed Jane's body next to Agatha on the settee, using string to fix Jane's cold, dead hand to Agatha's knee. Jane slumped. Agatha righted her, bearing her sister's weight without complaint.

Then came the tintypes. Four of them, all the same, before the family were forced to accept the impossible result: Orville and Hortense were slightly blurred, while Agatha's face was as sharp and clear as her dead sister's.

Even in death, the girls were inseparable.

"Is it true?" Amelia asked. "Was Agatha alive when the photos were taken?"

"Yes, but the consumption hit her hard. She was dead within a fortnight."

Amelia leaned closer, extending one lace-gloved hand. Her fingers stopped just short of Thad's arm. "Why do you suppose the camera predicted Agatha's death, but not the death of Orville's wife?"

Thad had often wondered that very thing. "I can only guess that Hortense's death was too far off. Somehow the camera, or whatever force had possessed it, or possesses it still…" He shook his head. "It couldn't see that far into the future."

Amelia withdrew her hand and nodded. "I think you must be right."

For the first time, Thad noticed the shadows hanging below Amelia's eyes—pale-blue half-moons that gave her the appearance of one who had gone too long without sleep.

"What do you want from me, Mrs. Temberly?"

She looked into his eyes. "I want you to take my portrait."

A dark foreboding sank in Thad's stomach like a stone in a lake. "Are you ill?"

"No."

"Afraid for your life, then?"

A nod.

He swallowed, the gravity of her request settling across his shoulders like a mantle. "I guarantee nothing," he said presently. "The camera has no special button to be pressed, no lever to be pulled. Agatha's portrait was both the first and the last."

"I understand."

"What if the result is... What would you do if you knew you were going to die?"

"Perhaps it would help if I started with *why.*" She gave a weak smile and smoothed a wrinkle from her skirt. "My husband, as you know, is preoccupied with oddities and artifacts. But his pursuit of such things has acquainted him with a darker obsession: the occult. When we're not exhibiting our collection, he's experimenting with death. He kills things, Thaddeus—mice, crows, rabbits, even dogs—and he brings them back to life. Or tries. His methods of revival have improved, but his success remains unpredictable. And unpredictability vexes him. It reminds him he is not in control."

"My God." The stone in his stomach tumbled in place. "In control of what?"

"The veil, of course. Now listen. Enoch is single-minded. He doesn't sleep. He is consumed by the idea that the dead will guide him in his dark pursuits. You see, only those who have traveled beyond the veil know its secrets. He performs séances, uses spirit boards, but it isn't enough. It's never enough." She paused. "Do you understand what I'm saying?"

Thad stared at Amelia, bile rising to his throat. *No... it can't be...it can't possibly be...*

"He wants an associate on the other side. Someone to reach back across the veil and assist him."

"You?"

She nodded. "He intends to kill me. I'm certain of it. I just don't know when."

The room began to spin, the gas lamp's guttering shadows opening and closing around him like a demon's wings. "You have to leave him, Amelia. You have to run!"

"Where would I go? I was nothing before he found me. No family, no money, nothing to my name. He saved me."

"But you could…"

"Live under a bridge? In a brothel?" She let out a low bark of laughter. "Anyone who says no fate is worse than death wasn't born a woman. Besides, who's to say Enoch is wrong? What if I *could* reach out to him from beyond?"

Thad buried his face in his hands.

"Please, Thaddeus. Take my portrait. I need to know how soon…"

He stood and began to prepare the the studio. He moved like an automaton, stiff and driven by habit, lighting lamps and positioning the camera on its tripod in the center of the floor. All the while, Amelia sat quietly on the settee, watching, waiting. He retrieved a fresh plate from the black room, prepared it, and loaded it into the camera, then ducked below the camera's drape to check that everything was in order.

At last, he stood beside the camera, fingers on the lens cap. "Take a breath," he told Amelia, "and hold as still as you can while I count to eight."

She obeyed. He counted. At eight, he placed the cap back on the lens. Pulling the plate from the camera, he said, "Wait here. I'll be only a few minutes."

"Thaddeus?"

He turned. In the lamplight, the half-moon shadows beneath her eyes seemed to have darkened to the same purple as her dress. "Yes?"

"Please know that whatever image appears, I will be fine. I just need to know."

Thad wished he could believe her. What could he say? She was married to an evil man. A necromancer. A practitioner of the occult. That was the life she had chosen. It was none of his business. Whatever image appeared, the knowledge it imparted would be hers and hers alone to act on as she pleased. It would have nothing to do with him. Nothing at all.

He was wrong.

The image materialized in shades of black and white and silvery gray. Amelia. On the settee. Every detail of her face—every lash, every lock of hair—as sharp and clear as the inanimate objects around her.

Perfect stillness.

Amelia Temberly was dead. But it was a horror quite different from her stillness that told Thad it was so.

He stumbled back into the water pump, flailed, knocked a bottle of developer from a shelf, heard it shatter on the floor. The plate slipped from his hand and landed with a metallic clank among the broken glass. He couldn't breathe. *God Almighty, he couldn't breathe.* His knees buckled. He slid to the floor.

And then, without warning, Amelia was there. She was *there*, in the black room with him, silent and shrouded in shadow.

She stooped to pick up the plate and regarded her portrait.

Her mouth opened in a soundless scream. One hand clutched at the slit that had opened her pale throat. Blood spilled between her fingers—the same blood that, in her portrait, drenched her bodice and the front of her corset.

She looked down at him, her lips endeavoring to form words but failing.

Thad staggered to his feet. "Enoch," he said. "He already killed you, didn't he? Earlier tonight, at the hotel."

Realization dawned in the dark pools of her eyes. She hadn't known until now she was dead.

"The séance," Thad continued. "It's for you. He's trying to contact you right now. He's reaching beyond the veil."

The fear in her eyes abated. Her hand fell away from her ruined throat, and she tilted her head as though listening. She smiled and closed her eyes.

Then she vanished.

⌒⌒⌒

The Georgetown sheriff arrested Enoch Temberly just before midnight. Thad was among the onlookers gathered in the street when Amelia's body, draped in a blood-soaked sheet, was carried out of the hotel. She was discovered after the man staying in the room below hers reported a red stain spreading across his plaster ceiling. Thad was relieved. How could he have explained his knowledge of Enoch's crime without implicating himself? It would have been quite impossible.

Some long, forgotten hour between midnight and dawn, Thad sat in his studio, alone and in the dark. He regarded the camera, still sitting atop its tripod in the center of the room. The camera was special. He knew that now, more than ever. Its lens could peek beyond the veil. It could see death before death swung its scythe. It could speak for the spirits who needed to see the truth of their demise. When focused on a proper subject, a subject in need, it could do good work. But it had a need of its own. A partner. Someone with a keen eye and a steady hand.

The camera needed *him*.

Given time, Thad could learn its use in the saving of lives. He could lay troubled spirits to their eternal peace.

Tomorrow, he would become more than a mere photographer. He would become the camera's steward. Tomorrow, his true work would begin.

❧

ANGIE HODAPP

Angie Hodapp has worked in language-arts education, publishing, and professional writing and editing for the better part of the last two decades. She is currently the Director of Literary Development at Nelson Literary Agency in Denver. She and her husband live in a renovated 1930s carriage house near the heart of the city and love collecting stamps in their passports.

HARRY AND MARLOWE VERSUS THE

HAUNTED

LOCOMOTIVE OF THE ROCKIES

CARRIE VAUGHN

1899

As they crossed the Great Plains of America, Harry was certain she'd never seen anything so astonishing in all her life.

The Kestrel hadn't had such a long stretch airborne since she crossed the Atlantic. Even on the third day of it, Harry leaned out a window to watch the land passing beneath them, and what seemed to be all of heaven passing above. "Have you ever seen the sky look so very large, Marlowe?"

"Only at twenty thousand feet of altitude."

Twenty thousand was nearly the upper limit of military-grade airship capabilities. Any higher, the air ran out. The sky was huge at altitude, but very lonely. According to the barometric altimeter, they were at some five thousand feet altitude now—only two thousand, vertical: Details of the ground spread out as on a map. Wind buffeted them, the sun blazed down. They might have been flying over an ocean, but this was grass, hundreds of miles of it, rippling with shadows and light. The yellowing plain seemed barren, featureless and undisturbed. Easy to become disoriented, when all directions looked the same.

The plains weren't really so desolate—at regular intervals, small towns grew up like weeds along the rail line. About a day's wagon trip apart, each of them. The Kestrel wouldn't be lost if something happened out here. Harry was almost sad about it—she didn't really mind the loneliness of being in an airship over an endless plain.

She had to search for it, but she picked out the double lines of the railroad tracks, along with accompanying telegraph wires on posts, that guided them on. Best way to navigate in such a place. Someone might have taken a pencil to a map. She followed the line west, where something like a mirage disturbed the sameness of the planes, a rough gray splotch, rising like some distant wall.

"Marlowe, you'll want to look at this," she said, nodding ahead.

A smile flickered on his lips as he made another small course correction, heading directly toward that gray shadow.

The Rocky Mountains.

❧

They stopped briefly in Colorado Springs, an oasis on the plains that was very nearly cosmopolitan. Pikes Peak rose like a tower to the west of the town, some fourteen thousand feet in altitude. The mountains were a wall marking the end of the plains, and they kept going, peak after peak. Traversing them in the airship would be a challenge.

They had a bit of a scare approaching the town. Marlowe squinted some distance south, and Harry took up the spyglass. Another airship, even smaller than the Kestrel, with an open gondola, traveled at an easy pace. Three men were on board.

"They're flying a U.S. Cavalry flag, I think," she said. "A local patrol, perhaps? That ship certainly isn't built for distance."

"I'd wondered if the cavalry would use airships out here. Best way to keep track of all this territory, I should think."

Sun glinted off the other gondola, a reflective flash. A man looking back at her through his own spyglass. "They're watching us," she said.

"Run up flags. I don't want to waste time explaining ourselves to them."

Naval semaphore flags worked just as well inland, and Harry raised the flags along their gondola that identified them as a private ship registered in Chicago. A lie, of course, but nothing would draw the attention of the U.S. Cavalry faster than if she raised the correct British Navy flags. Fortunately, the patrol vessel believed them and maintained its course north and east.

The Kestrel had drawn attention wherever she flew in America. Harry found herself avoiding the crowds as much as she could—a stray photograph of her placed in front of knowing eyes might reveal her true identity, and that wouldn't do at all. Her and Marlowe's roles here were part tourists, part spies, and part archeologists. Marlowe put himself forward as a research assistant to a member of the Royal Academy, gathering notes for a treatise on Aetherian technology outside of Britain. To preclude awkward questions, Harry was usually introduced as a relative of his along for the education. No one knew that she was also Princess Maud of Wales, and she hoped that if by some strange chance they met someone who recognized her, such a person would have the good sense to keep quiet about it.

They were searching for innovation. For something new. As was their wont, the Americans had taken Aetherian technology like locomotive engines and made them faster, cheaper, and more efficient. They had adapted the Aetherian engines to the paddlewheel ships that plied the Mississippi. They had also done things like build an entirely mechanical elephant, billed as Jumbo from the Stars, which currently performed in a specially built arena at a place called Coney Island.

So far, though, she and Marlowe had found nothing new, and no evidence that anyone had stumbled upon lost artifacts not part of the original Aetherian wreckage at Surrey.

In Colorado Springs, they obtained a set of local maps and identified their next destination: a small crossroads town in the mountains called Georgetown.

"Remind me: How did you discover this place?" Marlowe asked. He had the new maps spread out on the collapsible table set up in the middle of the cabin.

Colorado Springs had a number of hotels that were meant to be very fine, and Harry thought longingly of a hot bath and a dinner on fine china. But they hadn't indulged in New York, Baltimore, or even St. Louis, and they most certainly wouldn't indulge here. They were on campaign, as she thought of it. Better to maintain their cover as academics of only moderate means. When needed, a curtain divided the cabin into two makeshift rooms, and Marlowe was a model of propriety. On the other hand, she was an only partially successful aspirant toward propriety.

"A dime novel, would you believe?" she said. "'The True Story of the Haunted Locomotive of the Rockies.' I've got a copy stashed in my trunk if you'd like to see it."

"Are the illustrations very lurid? Then I might."

She dug in her trunk, stowed under one of the benches, and found the book, which indeed had an astonishing engraving on the cover: a locomotive with flames streaming from its coupling rods and a cattle guard in front stretching open like a fang-filled mouth.

Marlowe regarded the picture skeptically. "Are you telling me you've planned the next stage of this expedition based entirely on a story in a penny dreadful?"

That wouldn't have been the worst reason she'd offered for an expedition. "Not entirely. I also found some newspaper stories of accidents and strange goings-on, all involving this one stretch of rail out of this one town." She presented a newsprint clipping tucked into the pages of the book.

Marlowe read aloud. "'Three experienced engineers vanished into thin air after attempting to travel with the engine. Since then, no others have dared attempt the journey. The phantom train departs on schedule and returns on schedule . . . without any human guidance. The metal of the steel monster glows green in the dark.' Ah, I see."

She said, "I think someone made some improvised modification to an Aetherian engine and created something entirely new. Or perhaps someone has discovered some new artifact, some remains from an undiscovered Aetherian landing."

"Or it could all be a sensationalist tale from a dime novel."

"It could, but it's worth a look. And the stationmaster in Georgetown is offering a bounty for anyone who can disable the engine and stop the train. Four men have already vanished in the attempt—presumed dead, devoured by the monster engine. This is in addition to the three missing engineers."

"Good God, how can I turn down a challenge like that?"

She grinned. "I thought you'd say that."

❧

They reached Georgetown in a few hours of moderate flying the next day—the winds in the mountains were unpredictable, and Marlowe stayed alert at the helm. By then, Harry had to admit that any romantic notions she'd harbored about the American West were terribly

106

outdated. No stagecoaches in sight, no stampedes, no shootouts between marshals and bandits. Indians, identifiable from their shining black hair and brown skin, wore the same clothes as other citizens of the town: dungarees and button-up shirts. Unlike Colorado Springs, Georgetown was a small town, with one main street and a few brick and stone buildings.

The town did not have an aerial mooring. "It's the mountains, I imagine," Marlowe explained. "The winds are so intractable, trains are simply a more reliable form of transportation." He was clearly cross from fighting to keep the Kestrel level.

"Except when they're taken over by Aetherian ghosts," Harry said.

"Well, yes. What they really need out here are some German pilots to train them—all that practice flying over the Alps. Not that I'm going to suggest it."

Marlowe found an open lot outside of town where he could lower the Kestrel by partially deflating its bladder. They would not set down, but they could use a rope ladder to descend and anchor the ship via stakes in the ground. Marlowe climbed down with a bundle of long metal stakes and a hammer, while Harry threw him lines to tether the gondola.

A crowd had gathered to watch. People kept a respectable distance, shading their eyes to stare up at the balloon and the Aetherian motor, which, even powered down, gave off a hum and a glow.

A man detached himself and stepped forward, hesitant—perhaps because of the large hammer Marlowe was swinging. Time for Harry to intervene.

She wore a long divided riding skirt, a blouse and vest, good boots and gloves. Her hair was pinned up under a brimmed hat. Not her preferred ensemble for real work, but she had a feeling she'd need to look respectable while talking to nervous officials. She wondered if this man wore a brass star under his suit coat, or if that was another outdated romantic notion.

"Hello, there!" she called to him, climbing down the ladder, satchel over her shoulder. "I do hope it's acceptable that we moor here for a day or two. We'll pay a fee—rent for the land, if you like. We've got to purchase some supplies, and have some other tasks as well. My name is Miss Mills."

She stuck out her hand for shaking, giving him no chance to refuse. The man seemed just as startled by her as by Marlowe and the hammer, either because of her English accent, her forward manner, or both. But he'd brightened at the mention of money, as she'd hoped he would.

He was an older man with greying hair, but still fit of form. "Conrad Finch, ma'am. I'm the deputy mayor here. I gotta say, we don't often see airships at all, much less such fine . . . foreign . . . ones as this. With the war on in Europe, I'd have thought a ship like this would be in the fighting."

The man had a good eye—American ships tended to have open gondolas, unlike the solid closed gondola of the Kestrel, and Finch had probably never seen anything so modern as her very fine engine. She wondered how much he was really asking: Were they deserters? Had they stolen this ship from the Navy? Were they spies on some mission, or something else entirely? To a knowing eye, the Kestrel was certainly a military-grade vessel, for all that they'd disguised her with clumsy bags of ballast and unpolished brass fittings.

Harry entirely ignored the implied questions. "Pleasure to meet you, Mr. Finch. May I introduce James Marlowe, the pilot of the Kestrel?"

Marlowe let the hammer hang at his side as he finally came over to meet the locals. Watching the crowd, Harry saw him through their eyes: He looked exactly like an airship pilot should, with a leather jacket and scarf, tall boots, goggles pulled down around his neck, and a windburned glow to his stubbled face. As romantic as any heroic archetype the American West had produced. She sighed a little.

"I suppose you're wondering why we've come out all this way," Marlowe said.

"Well, I suppose so. Like I said, we don't get airships out here too often. What with the mountains and all." He gestured over his shoulder. The mountains were a barrier surrounding them.

"We'd like to have a look at that phantom locomotive of yours," Marlowe said, smiling a perfectly agreeable, innocent smile.

Finch's expression fell. If Harry had to name the distant look that had entered his gaze, she would have called it haunted. He spoke in the tone of someone announcing a death.

"You'll want to talk to Cooper."

❧

They determined ownership of the lot, negotiated and paid a reasonable fee, and even found a pair of trustworthy men to hire as guards. In fact, a handful of them argued for the honor, and Harry got a very good rate for their time.

Then it was off to see this train.

The train yard quiet. A chalkboard timetable hung in a waiting area, which was clean and inoffensive, if not terribly comfortable.

Outside, the sole locomotive had been adapted to run on Aetherian engines, and the modifications were entirely standard, nothing usual or noteworthy about them. Nothing growling or monstrous, as on the lurid engraving.

Finch found the stationmaster in an office toward the back, where a large window overlooked the yard. The office door stood open, and the trio of them, trailed by a few onlookers and other officials who'd not stayed behind to gawk at the Kestrel, trooped up to the threshold. The deputy mayor knocked on the doorframe.

"Cooper? These folks are here to try for the ghost," he said curtly, a sour look on his face.

A heavyset and overworked-looking man looked up from the cluttered desk where he sat, and with a sigh he stood and put on his suit jacket, which had been hanging over the back of his chair. His gaze fell on Harry, and an eyebrow raised in curiosity. Finch made introductions.

The stationmaster was simply Mr. Cooper, and as expected, he directed his statements at Marlowe. His expression was grim, his frown pulling down his sideburns. "Son, a dozen men before you have come here thinking they can tame that monster, and every one of 'em is dead. What makes you any different?"

"I'm British," Marlowe said, a wicked twinkle in his eye, giving Harry a sideways glance. "And I have the able assistance of Miss Mills."

Cooper looked them up and down and seemed on the verge of countering the challenge. He only shook his head. "Ma'am, with all due respect, you do not want to get involved with this thing."

"Oh, I think I do," she said calmly, not inviting argument.

Marlowe said, "I was hoping you could give us some more information beyond what's in the newspapers and penny dreadfuls."

Both Cooper and Finch shook their heads at that. "Damn that reporter—pardon me, ma'am—who came through. That book is going to be the only thing anyone remembers about Georgetown."

"When did the trouble start?"

Cooper sat heavily, and the others took up comfortable positions leaning on walls, arms crossed or hands in trouser pockets.

"Six months ago. Before that everything was fine, just fine. This train—it makes a run over the pass to Silver Plume and back. It's a local line, once a day, shouldn't be trouble. But one day the regular engine broke down, and we had one of the bug-rigged ones hanging around—"

"Bug-rigged?" Harry asked.

"Aetherian-adapted, I think," Marlowe said.

She had never heard the term before. It was amusing, appalling, and appropriate, all at once. God bless the Americans and their ornamental figures of speech. "Go on," she said.

"We hitched it on up to the regular train, mostly freight and a couple of Pullman cars. Five hours later, I get a telegram from the Silver Plume station wanting to know where the train is. Couple hours after that is when the train rolls back here. A dozen passengers stormed off, the driver was white as a ghost, but no one could say what happened. The thing got up into the mountains, into one of the tunnels, everything went dark, there was a bunch of noise, and when it came back out of the tunnel, it was . . . different. It's got, well, some kind of stuff on it." That haunted look again.

"I sent the train back on schedule the next day with another driver and a couple of guards. The train came back on schedule that afternoon. They didn't. No sign of trouble, it's like they just hopped off the train and sent it rolling back here. We haven't gotten anything through that line in six months. "

"And the company's done nothing to investigate?" Marlowe asked.

"Sure they have. Sent people up on horseback, checked the tracks, checked the tunnel. Watched the train—it stops in the tunnel and turns right back around, all by itself. Whenever we put a driver on it—the driver don't leave the tunnel. Can't get anyone to try again. So now we've got the bounty. You figure out what's happening up there, the railroad'll pay ten thousand dollars. But I'm not putting any bets on you."

Finch said, "Man with an airship like yours don't need ten grand, I expect."

"It's true. We're not here for the reward," Marlowe said. "We're here for the adventure."

"Then you're even crazier than I thought," Finch huffed. "Both of you."

Cooper pointed at Harry. "You're not getting the lady involved, are you? You're not taking her up the mountain?"

"Why wouldn't I go?" Harry said.

The stationmaster flustered. "Well. It's just. I—it's dangerous, ma'am. We've got a fine hotel here in town if you want to wait for your . . ." The word husband was on the tip of his tongue, until he evidently remembered their different last names. He didn't know what she was.

"I make my own choices, Mr. Cooper," she said.

"Train pulls in every day at noon. You want to take a shot, I won't stop you. It's never late. Wish all my trains kept their schedules like that. But we won't be held responsible for anything that happens to you," Finch said. "'Round here, we're used to folks heading into the mountains to prospect or whatnot, and never coming back. You won't get special notice."

Harry hid a smile, because they didn't know she was a princess of England, and if she vanished, someone would certainly give her special notice. "We understand. Thank you."

❧

Marlowe had that enviable Naval ability to claim sleep in the space of minutes, in any position, in any environment. He stretched out on the padded bench in the Kestrel's main cabin, and that was that. Harry tried to do the same in the pilot's chair, and failed. Their plan was in place—as much of a plan as they could make until they got their first look at the locomotive. Then they would board a machine that had evidently killed a number of men and made their bodies vanish.

She tried to imagine what they might see in that moment, but failed to conjure a picture.

"Harry," the lieutenant mumbled. "Try to sleep."

"Yes, I know," she sighed.

"There's nothing we can do until morning. You need to rest."

"Yes."

"There's a flask in the pouch behind the pilot's chair."

"I know where the flask is, Marlowe." A swallow of whiskey would, in theory, put her a step or three closer to sleep.

"Well then. You know your mind." A moment later, he was snoring softly.

Digging in the pouch hanging over the back of the chair, she found the metal flask and took the swallow. The drink warmed her, but it was still another hour before she got any sleep at all.

Harry wore trousers the next day, propriety be damned. Today, she had to be ready to move. Her boots were scuffed, her gloves worn, her jacket weather-stained. Anyone could see this was not her first time out in the world.

On the ground under the Kestrel, she secured her pistol in its holster at her hip. It was an Aetherian pistol, the kind Britain didn't export. It would be as rare a sight here as the Kestrel, but with luck no one would notice she had it. After she pulled her pack and coils of rope over her shoulder, she looked up at the ship and said a silent farewell.

"We'll solve this," Marlowe said, coming up by her shoulder with his own gear, instruments and tools slung in pouches on a bandolier and belt. "We'll be back at noon tomorrow."

"Yes," she said. "I know."

On the way out, Marlowe talked to their impromptu guards. "Do resist laying claim to her until you're sure we've failed to return on the noon train tomorrow, yes?"

The two men stammered and scuffed their toes, but they agreed to keep watch at least until then.

Cooper was waiting for them on the platform outside the station, pocket watch in hand. So was Finch, along with a crowd of townsfolk come to see them off. Gawkers. Harry might have wished for less publicity. They had five minutes until the phantom locomotive arrived.

"I feel like we're heading out to harpoon a whale," she murmured.

"Surely this won't be anything so dramatic. We take a look at the thing, board it if necessary, see where it takes us while examining and disabling the machinery. The men who've tried this before had little experience with Aetherian machinery. It's been waiting for us to come and speak to it in its own language."

"I do hope that was a metaphor."

"Here it comes," Cooper said, looking out along the tracks to the north. "Right on time."

No shrill, distant whistle announced the engine's approach. Only the clank of wheels against rail and the low, throbbing hum of an Aetherian drive emitting a great deal of power. The townsfolk who were present backed up, pressed themselves to the wall of the station as the beast slowed and came to a stop at the platform. It moved in reverse on this leg of the journey, pushing its coal car ahead of it. As Cooper had explained, the rest of the cars had been uncoupled, so only the engine and former coal car remained, a monstrous beast plying the tracks with a will of its own.

It didn't look like a steam locomotive fitted with an Aetherian drive, or even one designed with Aetherian technology from the first. This was something else entirely, and wholly unlike any machine Harry had seen. In an adapted locomotive, the Aetherian generator was typically built into the furnace, with tubes and pistons connecting the generator to the side rods along the engine's wheels. But while this engine might once have been a retrofitted steam locomotive, it had changed: Where the tubes and pistons connected the side rods along the wheels to the Aetherian generator, typically built into the firebox in such an arrangement, additional cabling looped around the broiler and into the cabin, growing almost organically in the manner of vines, obscuring the windows, stretching over the roof and reaching back. Wires tangled around each other over the coupler, swarming to the empty coal car, where the tips of the tendrils lay reaching out along the metal, waiting to extend further. All of it glowed a pale green, the familiar sickly, pulsing light that seemed to accompany all things Aetherian.

"Bug-rigged, indeed," Harry said.

"I've never seen anything like it," Marlowe breathed.

That gave Harry pause. She'd never heard Marlowe hesitate over anything, particularly where research was concerned. She had seen many of the same extreme Aetherian experiments he had. But this—was something else. "Marlowe, if you aren't sure—"

"No. Let's go. We'll alight on the coal car." The back half of the car remained free of Aetherian growths; the steel box seemed safe enough. Marlowe was still looking at the engine—something had caught his attention.

Stationmaster Cooper said, "You folks only have a minute to get on. If you're sure you want to do this."

"Thank you," Harry said. "We'll see you tomorrow then, yes?" Cooper just shook his head.

Harry and Marlowe kept hold of their ropes and wrenches, wire cutters and all the rest, and hopped on to the ledge at the end of the coal car just as the engine hummed to a higher pitch, reversed direction, and clacked back along the tracks, away from the station and toward the mountains.

❧

She had the feeling they had grabbed the tiger by the tail.

They settled on the narrow platform at the back of the coal car, keeping hold of a railing there, while the engine slipped through the yard and out of town. It ran smoothly, its hum almost out of hearing; all she heard was the rhythmic clanking of wheel on track. But the machinery before her was like the gaping maw of some fantastical creature.

Tubing and glowing wires looped out from the cab across the coupling to the coal car—the tender. The ends trailed off, fused to the steel sides. The tender itself was empty—unnecessary, once the engine had been convert-ed. Inside, the cab was filled with twisted mechanisms that seem to have grown rather than been built. The controls and levers had been obscured, only visible if you knew where to look. The door to the furnace was open, and the green of the Aetherian generator inside pulsed. Nothing came out of the chimney but an occasional green spark. As Cooper and Finch had said, there was no sign of a driver, an engineer, or anyone else. The thing was entirely autonomous.

Marlowe used his spyglass to study components of the engine. "I think—I believe much of the mechanism has grown from the original alterations. It's not unheard

118

of; some wiring from the Surrey crash seemed to have plant-like properties. Some samples kept sealed in a box were discovered years later to have grown. Nothing like this." He leaned out, keeping one hand on the railing, for a better look at the outside. "There—that's the standard retrofit. Everything else was added, and not by any known principles of Aetherian mechanics."

"So we're dealing with unknown principles. Is there some mad scientist in the hills making alterations, then sending the thing back? Murdering those who try to stop him?"

"An American mad scientist would be trying to patent the thing, I expect," he said.

"Then what if someone found a cache of Aetherian artifacts of unknown properties, introduced them to this engine, and got far more than they expected?"

He nodded. "If some prospector found a previously unknown Aetherian crash site in these mountains—well, anything could happen."

They were outside the town now, and the locomotive seemed to accelerate. They still had time to jump without being seriously injured. Soon they would reach the hills and mountains beyond. The sky overhead was searing blue. With no choking coal smoke pouring from the engine, she could smell fresh, chill air from the mountains.

Marlowe continued. "I expect what we'll find is some camp in the mountains. Someone's altered the engine with some new artifact they found, but they can't shut it down, and so it keeps running this route via some kind of automatic instructions built into this new wiring. When someone rides the train up, they're taken prisoner, and there you have your haunted locomotive."

"So what will we do when we get there, reason with them?"

"That's your job," he said archly. "For my part, I think I can disable the engine, just as soon as I find the nonstandard component. Remove it, see what makes it tick, get the thing back under control. I imagine our amateur engineer will be grateful."

They studied the weird mechanics grown in and around the cab, searching for that nonstandard component, that thing that didn't look familiar or right. Really, the entire locomotive was unfamiliar and wrong, so trying to find just one aberration was difficult. In fact, the more she looked, the more wrong it looked. Not just unsettling—no matter how much she and her world depended on Aetherian machinery, she'd always felt some discomfort around the more extreme examples—but deeply wrong.

Finally, Marlowe said, "I think . . . ah yes, that's new. There's a touch of red in the firebox. I thought it was overheated metal, but I think it's an independent source of radiation."

"Marlowe, let me see that a moment." She held her hand out, and he gave her the spyglass.

Stretching up, anchoring against the railing at the back of the tender, she looked through it, not at the mechanical parts of the engine, the glowing of the firebox—she saw the spot of red Marlowe mentioned, like a candle in a fogbank—and adjustments made to the valves and rods. She focused on the shadows inside the cab, on vague details hidden there.

A bit of red fabric, like from a kerchief worn about the neck, fluttered in a corner. A few feet beyond it, a tuft of brown hair sprouted from a pressure gauge. Near the roof was a hand, colored green as if grown over with moss, pierced through with glowing Aetherian wires.

Harry lowered the spyglass and settled on the platform. "Marlowe, I think we've got to get off this thing."

"Do you know how fast we're going?"

She spared a glance; the valley's grassy meadow slipped by in a blur. Trees of the forest ahead were now visible. They could no longer leave the train without being smashed on the ground.

She said, "Look in the cab, at the roof above the gauges."

He took the spyglass, and she pointed out the details she'd found, the odd human scraps among the alien whole.

"We've got to slow down at some point," he said.

"Yes, and we've got to stop the thing," she answered. "Before it kills us."

What had started as a treasure hunt, a search for new and unknown Aetherian artifacts to advance British supremacy, had become a bit more serious.

"We're already ahead of the game," he said. "The others—the unfortunate drivers, the bounty hunters who boarded later—all entered by the cabin. They thought to control the train from there. It would have been intuitive.

We've come at it roundabout. That gives us a little time, yes?"

Marlowe moved inside the coal car, braced up against the wall to shelter from the wind now whipping past the speeding train. Searching through the pouches slung over his shoulder, he gathered bits and pieces, wires and clamps. He obviously had a plan.

The air was growing cold. The train had entered a wooded stretch, and the mountains now rose up around them. Still, they were accelerating. How the train could navigate the mountain tracks at this speed, she didn't know.

He put a pair of needle-nosed pliers in his mouth while he fished for another piece out of a pouch. He was building something, right there amidst the rocking and shaking of the train. It had a lot of spiky bits and some kind of filament in the center that looked flammable.

"What exactly is it you're making?"

"A bypass . . . I think. To bleed off some of that power it's using."

They were roaring through the forest, moving faster than metal wheels on a metal track ought to be able to move. The trees passed by in a blur.

"Done," Marlowe said, shoving tools back into pouches and pulling himself to his feet. He held an object about the size of an apple, vaguely spider-shaped, with wires sticking out as legs, barbs at the tips looking like weapons. The body of it was a collection of loops and circuits and diodes. A filament glowed green with incipient power. "A bit of a prayer may be in order."

He then threw the device before Harry had time to make that prayer.

It sailed straight and true into the cab and stuck on one of the growths, a bottle-thick metallic coil pressing out against the walls. The barbed feet dug in, a crackle of energy burst from the device, sending green sparks throughout the cab. The invading growths seemed to flinch.

In just a second, the hum of the engines, as well as the sickly glow, increased.

"Marlowe," she murmured, drawing her pistol from its holster. He looked up at what had caught her attention.

The organic mound of machinery that had sprawled from the cab into the coal car had begun to move. Not quickly, not purposefully. It was more that it throbbed, as if some burrowing thing was making its way underneath the coiled and twisted surface. At the edges of the mound, wires emerged, sprouting out from the steel, stretching toward the newcomers, the invaders.

Aiming her pistol low, she fired across the front of the mound, the beam of energy frying the tendrils before they could progress further. The coiled mound shuddered, drew back. The humming of the engine took on a low, rough undertone, almost a growl. The light in the firebox flared red.

"I don't think your trinket bypassed much of anything," she muttered.

"Well, I tried," he said, put out.

She lurched, falling against the side of the car. They hadn't hit anything; the train was on a straightaway—no sharp turns ahead or behind. But the metal underneath her feet was moving.

The sides of the coal car bowed outward. The roof of the cab had swelled, and the cab's windows warped into gaping circles. The very steel of the original train was expanding. Not melting, because there was no heat, but somehow the structure of the metal was changing as the Aetherian coils mounded inside the cab grew, puffed up, and expanded outward. In the cab, pieces of bodies bloated outward, and they looked as if they had been eaten, skin flayed, bone pocked with holes, blood entirely drained. The monster might have been sucking them for more power, using them to become ever larger. The bounty hunters who'd come to tame the beast had only helped it grow.

Meanwhile, Harry fired again at the snaking tendrils creeping toward them. Again, the locomotive growled in displeasure.

Marlowe's device continued sparking bolts of green energy—diverting the locomotive's power, as he'd explained. The engine coughed, and Harry felt a surge of hope that whatever was driving the train would be disabled. She watched Marlowe for his reaction—his gaze was grim, watchful. He did not seem optimistic.

The entire train, engine and coal car, bucked, and Harry was sure they'd jumped the tracks and were about to crash—which in her estimation would be a good thing, given the alternative. But no, the vehicle had literally shivered, like a horse dislodging a fly. Marlowe's spider came loose from its anchor, slipped off the train, in between the two cars and onto the tracks where it was surely smashed to pieces. The strange red glow from the firebox pulsed.

"What now?" Harry breathed.

"I don't know."

That was worrying.

The crawling tendrils were increasing in size—and speed. She fired at the front line again and again—then shouted at a pressure on her wrist, her off hand, which was gripping the railing at the end of the car. A tube made of some rubberized, flesh-like stuff coiled around her wrist. She fell back, yanking away, but the tube only squeezed more tightly. Bringing her pistol around, she aimed some distance away along the undulating thing and fired. The tube flinched—squeezing yet tighter—and a stray charge from the ray blast traveled up the tube and tingled through her arm. Shivering at the shock, she blinked, shook her head, and tried to figure out what to do about this. Her hand was numb, immobile.

She slammed the butt of her pistol against a coil of tube lying against steel. No effect.

Behind her, Marlowe grabbed hold of her. She leaned into him as far as she could, giving him room to reach around with a very sharp-looking tool, like forceps with probes on the end. He stabbed this into the tube a few inches from where it held her, and the probes let off arcs of green energy. The tube went limp, and Harry quickly scraped it off her hand. The whole length fell to drag behind them on the ground.

"Are you all right?"

125

She had to open and close her hands a few times to get feeling back. "Yes."

Ahead of the speeding train, a towering rock face loomed. "Marlowe, look!"

This was the tunnel Cooper had mentioned, a place where blasting through the solid granite of the Rockies had been deemed easier than going around. As they watched, leaning out from the car, the stone unfolded.

The tunnel would have looked normal to the riders who'd come to investigate. They'd have seen nothing wrong with the tracks, with the gaping mouth of the hole blown out of the mountainside or the rough granite within. But at the train's approach, the stone changed, expanded, throwing out tendrils and wires, turning the stone into an alien maw. A match for the modified mechanics of the locomotive, the tunnel seemed designed to swallow the train.

"We can't let the train enter that tunnel," Harry said.

"There—that red light that keeps flashing from the firebox," Marlowe said. "That's what we want."

The light seemed to come from a specific point, a globe emitting the glare like a light bulb. It flashed every time they did something to the engine—every time they made it angry.

"Do you have any idea how to accomplish this?"

He shrugged. "I'm not sure. But I would like to keep it intact if we can."

To study it, of course. Exactly their mission. "And how do we do that?"

"We must get inside, of course."

She pursed her lips and considered. "Well. How about I create a distraction?" She looked around, found her footing. Hauling herself up, she braced one boot against a railing and the other against the top edge of the coal car, one of the few spaces not yet overrun with the writhing mechanism. But the tendrils were coming closer, climbing up the sides, stretching out with their eyeless certainty.

Her balance on this perch was imperfect. In moments, she'd either be grabbed by the alien machine, or would be knocked off when the train came into contact with its partner at the tunnel.

She aimed her pistol over the locomotive, around its chimney, to the undulating walls of the tunnel reaching out to her. Firing, she kept her finger on the trigger and swept a steady beam across the machinery. The massed coils shuddered, flinched—and continued reaching out.

She spared a glance—Marlowe had taken to using brute force: a crowbar he'd stashed in his bag. He pried tubing out of his way, whacked at a bundle of wires writhing toward him, stabbed at an undifferentiated mass of machinery that had grown up over the coupling.

Meanwhile, the train slowed. Coils of bronzed wires reached up from the rounded sides of the engine to join with the coils reaching down from the tunnel, and the two sets twisted together, pulling the locomotive to a gentle stop, like an airship coming to rest against its mooring platform. A mollusk folding into its shell. In this new incarnation, the locomotive was home.

At the edge of the tunnel, the wire tendrils radiated from a central point, much as the locomotive's adaptations grew from the firebox. That—that spot was key, and needed to be disabled as much as the light in the firebox did. She glanced at Marlowe's progress; he was spending so much time battling the crawling mechanism, he had no chance to go after his target.

They had to do something drastic soon, or they would be overwhelmed, swallowed up by that alien mouth, just as those who had come before them had been.

"Marlowe—I'm going to try to give you an opening. Be ready!" Arms out for balance, she made her way along the edge of the coal car, from the untainted steel to the part of the train that had been overwhelmed with the Aetherian intrusion. Approaching the roof of the cab, she reached up and let a draping tentacle grab hold of her. Coiling around her left arm, writhing like a snake, it pulled her off her feet, raised her into the air.

"Harry!" Marlowe called.

"Go, just go!" she called back. He scrambled over the mound of gross mechanics and into the locomotive's cab. Once he was under the roof, she could no longer see him. She turned her attention forward.

She kept her other arm, the one holding the pistol, low and out from her body where she hoped it would not be bound up in the coils. The thing had hold of her body now, squeezing her legs and torso with a constant pressure. It wasn't painful—as if it knew she was a living thing and had no wish to harm her. And yet it was drawing her inexorably upward, into its central maw.

That was her target.

This was a matter of timing: She had to maintain her range of motion and some semblance of calm when she reached that central point. But the number of tentacles locked on to her was increasing. Indeed, more seemed to come into being before her eyes. Soon, the thing would envelop her completely. She lunged.

Using her very bonds as leverage, she thrust forward her right hand, stabbed her pistol as far into thing's root as she could—the distance was considerable, more than she was expecting, because there was no central mass. The thing resembled a ball of yarn, threads coiled endlessly upon one another. The mass of threads pressed against her, seeking to immobilize her.

While she still could, she fired the pistol in the beast's heart.

There was an explosion, and she fell.

The tentacles all loosened at once, releasing her at the precise moment she was high in the air with nothing below to break her fall.

The pistol was gone, destroyed. Hands free now, she grabbed one of the flailing tubes. It held, and she swung, smacked against the granite mouth of the tunnel—but it was just a tunnel now, with strange metallic vines hanging over the entrance. No longer a mouth. Her right arm ached—the blast from the gun and subsequent explosion had shredded her glove and the sleeve of her jacket. The fabric had only partially protected the skin underneath, which was pocked with cuts and bleeding.

Below, the train had stopped. She still couldn't see Marlowe in the cab. Hanging from her length of metal, she waited, watched for movement. Didn't see any.

"Marlowe!" she called. No answer. "Marlowe! James!"

"Yes?" He emerged, straddling the coupling between cars, looking up at her. He had the crowbar and pliers in one hand, and something odd and alien in the other.

She slumped, relieved, and lowered herself down the vine until she was resting on the roof of the cab. Here, too, the Aetherian appendages seem to have died in place. She pushed them away, and they dropped to the ground. "This is entirely bizarre," she said.

"Yes. What do you think of this?" He handed her the thing he was holding, the component from the firebox.

It was hexagonal in shape, the size of her two hands together, and heavy. An intricate network of tiny wires ran across it in a mind-breaking geometric pattern. Given time, she might make sense of it, but at the moment it seemed a blur. She had trouble focusing on it.

A reddish glow suffused the device, and several prongs around the outside of it were probably connectors. It was meant to be attached to something else. Somehow, it had made its way into the firebox and found a home there.

"Just a moment," she said, looking back up at the cavity where she'd discharged her pistol.

She grabbed back hold of the tentacle she had climbed down on. It slipped, dropping—starting to come loose. Her arm was bleeding more profusely, the lacerations unhappy with her exertions, but she ignored the discomfort. Carefully so as not to dislodge the vine further, she climbed, bracing her boots against segments of material that had grown together.

Back at the edge of the tunnel's mouth, she could examine the tentacles here further. She drew her knife out of its belt sheath. She couldn't cut through the metallic tendrils and coils, but she could pry apart the segments, and the metallic appendages dropped away, giving her better access to the hollow place in the rock from which the tendrils emerged. Almost a cave, tucked away where no one could see it.

She traded the knife for a hand lantern from her belt pouch and examined the interior. The surface was scorched, stripped and burned by the pistol blast. But yes, there was a space, and inside were the scattered and melted remains of her pistol and a device much like the one Marlowe had shown her. She collected the pieces, tucking them into her pouch. They were still warm.

She dropped back onto the roof of the cab, then across the coupling and into the coal car, where Marlowe was clearing away tentacles and segmented tubes. The locomotive was appearing more like its old self and less Aetherian monster, by the moment.

"I think there must have been a cave or some pocket in the mountain side," she said. "It might have been covered by debris until the rail company came along and blasted the tunnel. An Aetherian craft or being might have stashed away some artifact, by chance or intent. Maybe they meant to retrieve it later. When it was exposed, it was activated somehow."

"Harry, you're hurt," he said.

She glanced at her arm. "Yes, but I think it just needs a bit of washing off—"

"No. Here, sit." He took her arm and guided her down to sit at the edge of the car. He touched her forehead; his glove came away bloody. She realized that throbbing wasn't nerves or the noise of the explosion rattling in her brain. She'd been cut by a bit of shrapnel.

"How bad is it?" Now that she noticed it, blood seemed to be running down her face. She didn't have time for this.

His expression furrowed as he leaned in to look, producing a handkerchief to dab at the mess. "You may need a stitch or two."

"My grandmother will never forgive me if I've ruined my face," she muttered.

He chuckled. "Not possible, Your Highness. Here, hold that." He gave her the handkerchief to press over the wound.

His touch lingered, resting on her chin a moment as he turned her face and seemed to study her eyes very intently. He was quite close, and her heart raced a bit. She would not lean in, not even a millimeter.

"Your pupils are the same size," he said. "Can you follow my finger?" He held up a hand and tracked it up, down, left, right. Obediently, her gaze followed the movement. "I don't think you're concussed, so that's good."

"Yes, very good," she murmured. Her chin felt cold when he finally let her go.

"Your hypothesis seems reasonable," he said. "Given what I think this might be."

He set the device from the firebox in the open. She produced the pieces she had retrieved, laying them alongside. Difficult, trying to make out what the thing had been. Whatever energy or glow it had was gone now, but the same complicated pattern of minute wiring was visible on some of them. They were a matched set. The intact device pulsed a little when the pieces came along side it.

"I think," Marlowe said, "that these are a set of devices to create automation in machines. Self-directed automation."

"It's . . . a mechanical brain?"

"If you like."

"Then you're saying it was alive."

He paused, furrowed his brow. "I don't know that I would go that far. The thing needed a machine to control. The locomotive came along. You remember what Cooper said, they'd switched a steam engine for an adapted one—bug-rigged. Like called to like. The artifact might also have had some component to defend itself. Hence our poor victims down there."

Defense—a weapon that could defend itself? Oh, this was dangerous indeed.

"But it had a will?" she asked. "Was it intelligent or merely carrying out some . . . artificial instinct? Like the German's mechanized troops?" Comforting, to think this was simply another version of the same kind of controls that operated the fearsome mechanical beasts that the Germans sent into battle. But this . . . this had been something more. The alien-controlled locomotive had seemed to have intent. No one had set the train on its path. No one human.

He tucked the device in a pouch and gathered up the pieces Harry had found—placing them in an entirely different pouch. "You wanted to make this expedition to learn more about Aetherian technology, to discover Aetherian mechanisms no one has seen before. I think we've succeeded here."

"But what are we going to do with it?"

"For now—lock it away and carry on."

They spent the rest of the afternoon clearing the train of its extraneous additions, stashing tentacles and coils of wire—and human remains—in the coal car. Marlowe was able to bring the original Aetherian-adapted engine back to functioning order. The thing hummed normally, and its green glow was exactly the shade it should have been. They spent the night camped by the tracks and didn't sleep very well. In the morning, they set off back to town. Without its brain, the locomotive was simply another Aetherian-adapted train, clacking mundanely as it ran back toward Georgetown.

They arrived back at the station at eight in the morning, four hours ahead of schedule. Mr. Cooper was waiting on the platform, all astonishment.

"We'll be collecting your bounty, I think," Marlowe said, cheerfully hopping onto the platform after shutting down the engine and letting the locomotive roll to a stop. Harry followed more slowly, aware of her bandaged head and arm and the stares she was attracting.

"What? How?" Someone had sent for Finch and several other town officials as well. They lined up like a jury, staring.

"Very carefully," Harry said. "And you'll need to call an undertaker."

They got the bounty, which seemed ridiculously anti-climactic to Harry, since they hadn't done any of this for money, and what she had seen was so much larger than mere money. But they had to maintain their cover story. Harry put her foot down and insisted they use part of the bounty to take rooms in the Hotel de Paris. They ate a very nice hot meal, drank the establishment's best bottle of wine—a mediocre burgundy—and had very hot baths. The next morning found them back at the Kestrel. They spent an hour or so packing before unmooring her lines. Harry was uneasy.

"Was it alive? Not just alive—but had the Aetherian pilots somehow left a piece of mechanical intelligence behind? A piece of themselves?" She couldn't stop asking the question. Her bandages itched, and resisting scratching them was making her cross.

Marlowe sighed. "Yes, it probably was alive, at some level. It grew, it had self-motivation. But I'm not sure it was any more intelligent than an earthworm. It was a machine, Harry. Whatever else it could do, it was mechanical."

"I can't help feeling that we have broken something that can never be repaired."

"It was trying to kill us, don't forgot."

"Yes. But I wish . . . Well. If it had been truly intelligent, we could have found a way to talk to it, yes? I would have liked to talk to it."

They finished stowing gear in the chests and cupboards on the Kestrel. The pieces recovered from the phantom engine got their own locked chest—far away from the Kestrel's engine. After checking the engines and gauges, examining the bladders for tears, repairing the one or two they found, they filled the bags with gas and pulled up stakes and lines. Marlowe climbed the ladder as the ship rose. A crowd of locals looked on with gaping curiosity. Some of the children waved, and Harry didn't wave back. The engine pulsed and whined, sent a fresh surge of gas into the bladder overhead, and the ship rose, up and up until the buildings below looked like toys made out of balsa.

"Where do we go from here?" she asked.

"West," Marlowe said, looking in the direction to where the sun would set in another six hours. "Always west."

∽✦∽

CARRIE VAUGHN

Carrie Vaughn is the *New York Times* bestselling author of the *Kitty Norville* urban-fantasy series as well as a Hugo-nominated writer of short stories. She is also a regular contributor to George R. R. Martin's and Melinda M. Snodgrass' *Wild Cards* series.

ARGENTINE PASS

STEPHEN GRAHAM JONES

2014

Jenny—

You're going to think I'm ragging on Shooter again, and that's fine. You're going to tell me I don't have any claim to you or your happiness and all that anymore, and you're right. You're going to say I'm just trying to get into your head since the wedding's tomorrow, and, sure, okay, whatever gets you listening to this message, okay?

If I'm being honest here, I am trying to get in your head. I do care about your happiness. And I know there's no chance of us ever picking up again. Let me just be clear as I can on that.

You can't marry Shooter, though.

You cannot marry him.

You're not supposed to see him all day today, right? That's the rule? So, when you do see him, he's going to be all tuxedoed up and probably three or four sheets to the wind, just to get through a ceremony where he has to avoid fighting with your dad or your brothers, and you can write off the stiff way he's acting as nerves.

It's not nerves, Jenny.

I know nerves. I've got nerves right now, making this call. I've had them since we came back down to Georgetown this morning. Shooter's out at the jeep right now smoking a cigarette and—and respooling the winch, yeah, but any moment he can be standing right in front of me again, hearing me tell you this, looking into my eyes like he's seeing my soul.

So, this is going to last about exactly until I see him tossing his butt into the street and crossing to the front door.

I'll go fast.

You knew that for his bachelor party he didn't want all the usual junk like from TV. He just wanted one last crawl with his boys—with me and Lex and Jolly Roger. You probably know Rog just as Roger, but on the trail, in the CBs, he's Jolly Roger, like his license plate. Don't worry about it, it's stupid.

I'm Kevin Spacey, if that helps any. The "spacy" is because of that time I wasn't paying attention, hung a wheel off into space.

Anyway.

Two jeeps, Lex's beat-up but bulletproof Toy, a cooler of beer, and jerry cans of gas strapped all over, and we were gone. One last weekend. One last crawl.

Because last time we'd tried Argentine it had been flowing water halfway up even Lex's door—Shooter'd been the only one with a snorkel on his rig, then—that's the turn we took. That's the trail we hadn't beat together, all three of us. And it would be faster to the top, really. The first trail, off Georgetown proper, it's a slowdown, with all the rockslides. Since Rog's JK is the family model with four doors, that means he'll high center if you let him. So we'd be winching him over those rockslides.

Argentine was supposed to be faster.

I was riding with Shooter for it. Not because my rig was up on blocks, and not because I trust his hand on the throttle more than mine, but because this was the last time, the last crawl, right? It always feels kind of lonely, each of us in our own ride, just daisy-chained along the trail.

I'm sentimental. Sue me. I've been knowing Shooter since fourth grade, though, and after you married him I was going to be having plenty of rides with me on my lonesome in the driver seat. I didn't mind leaving my Cherokee at the curb for this one time.

I keep telling you stuff you don't care about, sorry.

Just—I mean, you were there when we left, and you've seen us drive off for the weekend twenty other times at least. You know what it's like.

I know you like us going up the mountain, too. There's no bars up there. No other women.

I understand. You've been burned before, and I'm not unguilty.

That's all over and done, though. And this isn't about that anyway.

Two days ago. Friday.

Argentine Pass.

I know Shooter's taken you up before, with a tent, with his special tent, but I don't know if he talks the same while easing up the trail.

He has this thing he does where he says aloud what the trail must have been like a hundred years ago.

When I met him in fourth grade? That was two years before you got here. Back then, though, before girls, you could not keep Shooter Grafton out of the museum. Something about the old tools, the yokes, all of that. Every year at the parade, with the covered wagon and the horses?

He'd pretend it was just another sort-of float. But I could tell his heart was swelling in his chest.

I don't think he got into rock crawling for the jeep aspect, I mean. I think he got into for the being alone up there. It lets him feel like the mountain man he always thought he should have been. Me, I like the nuts and bolts of crawling, I like having to fix something when you don't have any of the right parts, and Lex, he's always taking pictures for his Instragram, like that's his job, and Rog—you know Roger. He just likes to sit somewhere and smoke out.

Shooter, though, I think he still fashions himself a pioneer. Just, one born too late.

When you ride with him, he'll talk through all the reading he's done about this ranch, that silver mine, this one town that's not there anymore, except in his head.

After we turned off onto Argentine—it wasn't flooded anymore, was barely enough to wet the tires—Shooter kept leaning forward over the steering wheel, pointing ahead with his chin.

"See him?" he'd say.

The first couple of times I fell for it, leaned forward to look. But we were the lead vehicle, the head of the centipede. There wasn't going to be anybody in front of us.

"His name's Marston," Shooter said, real contemplative like. "Either that or Marswell. Nobody's really sure."

When I stole a glance over at him, he had the face on he had for fourth grade, at the museum. He was in the past. This was someone he'd read about. Someone he was squinting into existence.

"You think that's a deer tied across the pommel of his saddle, don't you?" he went on. "There were no tags back then. None of this either." He gestured down at Argentine, which had tire tracks on it from whoever'd been up a day or two ago.

"Marswell," I said, tasting the name, trying to hear it like he was.

"Or Marston," Shooter said. "The old timers weren't really sure, just had the story from their dads and uncles. But they'd come across him way up in the trees every few months, just going from here to there like they used to."

"And he'd have a deer on his saddle?"

Shooter smiled, switched hands on the wheel to use the throttle, grind us up and over a hump.

It was all second-nature. A trail as untechnical as Argentine, you don't even have to think.

He kept his eye on the rearview, though, just in case Jolly Roger was already toking up, not paying attention.

Rog made it, of course. I like American steel, but I've got to give it to his little Toyota: It can get up and over with the best of us, especially the way he's got it tricked out.

After Rog, we were off the hook for watching, could keep going. It's only ever your job to keep an eye out for your immediate trailer—the next segment of the centipede.

"That's just it," Shooter said, looking over to be sure I was listening close for this, "Marston, it would *look* like a deer behind him on his horse. That's what you're expecting to see. And then, he always had like buckskin draped over it, so you'd double-think it was just a doe he'd popped."

Shooter squinted at a boulder leaning out into our path, eased around it close enough that the body armor had to grind it out.

"Story was," he said, "story was that sometimes you'd see a woman's hand or her foot coming out from under that buckskin. But it wouldn't be polite to say anything about it."

"Or safe," I added.

"Or safe," Shooter agreed. He nodded ahead of us, like we were moseying along behind Marston or Marswell and his dark cargo.

"The story people who encountered him let themselves believe, it was that they'd come up on him while he was delivering a loved one to a burial site. A wife, a sister, a daughter. Except no secret cemetery ever turned up."

"How many loved ones we talking?" I asked.

"Years of them," Shooter said, and smiled.

It's good to be born into the age of jeeps.

Or, before last night, I thought it was.

The whole way up all the twists and turns of Argentine, Shooter playacted like we were plodding along behind a horse's ass. That there was a Marston or a Marswell ahead of us on that horse, looking back now and again, his ratty hat brim pulled low, his face dirty behind that. Dirty and smiling.

It gave me the chills. I'm not proud. Shooter could do that to you.

It was getting dark, too. Our general plan, it was to find a turn-out, huddle up there for the night, let Rog unpack the night's recreational substances from the stash in his toolbox. We all had our headlights off, spotlights on. Way below, you could see 70. It was just a smear of halogen, most of it headed east, to get sucked into Eisenhower Tunnel.

Seeing all the glowing ants down there, it reminds you how high up you are.

Because it let Shooter feel more alone—more a mountain man—we'd eased ahead maybe a quarter mile from the Jolly Roger, which, at four and five miles per hour, is a bit of distance.

"Kill the head, the body will die," Shooter muttered, about the centipede we were supposed to be.

It turned out to be the other way around.

That's what I'm telling you, Jenny. That's why you can't go through with the ceremony.

Your fiancé is about to die.

143

I'm serious. You'll think I'm joking, that I'm lying, but I don't care.

I saw it happen.

We'd come up on a rockslide that was mostly gravel. We could have backed up, got some speed, just vaulted right over it, but up on a ledge-road like this, coming down that hard could crumble everything away right under you, and then you're cartwheeling down the side of the mountain, and you don't stop until eight or ten thousand feet later, when you hit a guardrail on 70.

So Shooter set the brake, stepped down—the doors were off like they are now—walked up to the winch.

I scooted over into the driver's seat and let the winch out, giving him slack. He walked ahead with it through the headlights.

There was some brush we could see peeking up over the mound of the slide. It wouldn't be enough for a real pull, but we didn't need much, just enough to keep the thirty-fives from spinning out in the loose stuff. We had the air pressure down in them already, like you do, but that mostly only helps with grabbing onto rock, not shale.

Shooter raised his hand for me to hold, hold, and then he squatted down to tie off. Where he was hooking into, once the winch pulled back, the cable was going to cut into the top of the mound, but it was soft, and who cared, right?

He had a beer in his hand, I had one between my legs, and life was good.

Until it wasn't.

I tightened the winch and eased the hand-throttle out together, the nose of the jeep crawling up the mound, and everything was perfect, everything was just like a hundred times before. I wouldn't doubt if he did this exact maneuver with you when you were up here. I'm not saying it was his move, but, I mean—let the girl get behind the wheel, let her climb over something while the guy's out there working the cable, guiding this way and that, and it's like the kind of couple you are, it just notched up a bit.

Except the cable snapped.

It's rated for twelve-thousand pounds, sure, and the jeep maybe went thirty-five hundred, counting me, but shit happens.

If anything, I would have expected the anchor to give, for the whole bush to come swarming over the top of the rockslide.

There must have been a burr on the winch rollers, though, I don't know. Some nick we'd picked up on the climb. Just enough to snap the cable at the jeep.

It shot forward like a bullet, and I saw—I saw with my own eyes, Jenny—I saw the ragged end of that cable slice across Shooter's face.

It sent him stumbling back along the ridge of that slide.

At the drop-side of it, he teetered, but just for a moment.

Then he was gone.

I was out of the jeep before the kill-switch had even activated. It was rolling away behind me, and I was

145

running, I was scrambling up the slide, I was reaching down into space.

Shooter was gone.

The brush and the darkness and the fall and swallowed him.

He was with the mountain, now. In the crotch of some tree, more bones cracked open than not.

Thirty seconds later, Rog and Lex and were there screaming and falling to their knees and using ropes and the other winches to lower Lex down the side of the mountain like repelling.

There was no chance. Even if the cable hadn't split his face, it was steep enough where we were that there was no hope.

At the end of that forty-five minutes, Roger ran to the ledge with our whole big cooler and dumped it all down after Shooter, and nearly went over himself. The cooler tumbled down and down, and then was gone.

"Search and rescue," Lex said, solemnly.

He was right. Except, in cases like this, it's more search and recovery.

Just bring a scaffold and some rope to haul the body back up.

I was sitting on my butt in the road, the headlights burning one side of me, my hands in my hair.

He was my best friend, Jenny. I mean that. I was happy for him and you, I really was.

And, even though our cells were all with different carriers, we were in some dead spot, couldn't dial up any signal at all. We tried the emergency band on the CBs, trying to snag some trucker down on 70 who could relay our call, but they're all blue-toothed into their cells these days keep their CBs dialed down quiet.

Nobody picked up.

Finally Lex—he's been the centipede's tail—turned around the spotlights he had mounted on his rollbar and reversed slow enough that we could follow him.

We weren't coming all the way down Argentine at night—one dead didn't mean we all had to die—but we needed a flat place to pitch a tent, anyway.

Rog didn't even smoke up. And all our beer was gone.

Lex was crying softly. He wasn't taking any pictures.

I was at Shooter's jeep, trying to clock what happened with that cable.

As near as I could tell, it was nothing. Bad luck. The worst luck.

I walked up to the rockslide for one last look, one last chance, and when I came back two hours later, my eyes swollen, the knuckles of my right hand packed with gravel and blood, Lex and Rog were still sitting by the fire.

And one of us was squatted down at the front of Shooter's jeep, studying the snapped-off cable.

"*Ho!*" I said. It was for Lex and Rog.

Shooter looked up from the winch and smiled as best he could, with a wide scab diagonaled across his face from the cable.

I ran to him, hugged him until he fell down, and didn't care how stupid I was being. Lex and Rog fell in and I think we were all crying.

Tough guys at the bachelor party, yeah.

We'd thrown all the beer down the mountain, but Rog still had his stash. We got pretty loose, pretty happy. It was a fucking celebration, Jenny. Shooter was *alive*. He'd grabbed onto some scrub, some root, and bellied down until he could crab across, finally walked back uphill way on the other side of the slide, until he found a game trail. It finally delivered him back to us.

It made sense. Also, when your dead friend's back, I think you'll believe anything, pretty much.

I passed out the vienna sausage I kept for emergency and Lex and Rog rigged sticks, cooked theirs over the fire. I ate mine raw, like you always hated. Shooter wasn't hungry yet, he said.

"I just died," he said. "Give me some time to work up an appetite, yeah?"

We ate and we laughed and we toasted him with the many joints of the Jolly Roger, and then, like always, we slumped over into something like sleep but a lot more like satisfaction.

When I woke, it wasn't from any sound or any non-sound. It was because I wasn't sure if I'd set the emergency brake on Shooter's jeep or not.

There were trees all around where we were, so it couldn't roll away or anything—and why would it start rolling in the first place?—but it was my responsibility.

I cracked an eye, stretched my chin to clear my throat, keep from coughing. I didn't want to wake the rest of them. I just wanted to keep them safe. Nobody wants to wake with a thirty-five on their head.

I wasn't the only one awake, though.

Across the embers from me there were the two lumps I knew were Lex and Rog, conked, their chest rising and falling.

Shooter should have been just shy of Rog.

He wasn't.

I tilted my head a bit, cased our campsite for if he was peeing, or smoking, or working on his scab in the dome light of Rob's truck.

You're not going to believe this, Jenny, and he'll just laugh it off if you ask, but he was—he was right out at the edge of the light from the embers of our fire. I know we're supposed to put it out, that the whole mountain can burn, but if we had put it out, I wouldn't have seen what he was doing.

Digging.

Not with the big shovel clamped onto his spare tire rack, but with the little fold-shovel that clipped into the back side of his tailgate.

He'd been going for an hour or two, it looked like. Judging by what he'd dug up already.

Four of what I at first thought were volleyball sized rocks.

They were skulls, Jenny.

Those old timers talking about Marswell or Marston always packing women up into the trees, they said they'd never found any secret cemetery, any high-altitude graveyard.

It was because there weren't any markers.

Shooter didn't need any markers, though.

Because he'd died. Up there on Argentine, at eleven thousand feet.

149

And when he came back, he knew where the bodies were buried.

You tell me what to do with that, Jenny.

If I were brave, if I were the hero of this story, I'd have waited until he leaned back over his digging. I'd have sneaked over behind the wheel of his jeep, fired it up, and put it into gear in the same instant, flooding him with enough light to blind him and then plowed into him, kept the pedal down into both of us launched out into the void.

But I'm no hero.

What I did was try to control my breathing, and then close my eyes, convince myself I'd been dreaming. Insist that, if I peeked out again, his face wasn't going to be right in mine.

And I kept pretending, Jenny.

All the way until morning. All the way down the mountain.

All the way until fifteen minutes ago.

Our trail-crates, mine and Shooter's, they're both grey bodies with yellow lids. You know them. He keeps his right inside the garage, so he can up the mountain at a moment's notice. We bought them together at the hardware store, ten dollars a pop.

I'd hauled mine into my house instead of his, see.

I can't pretend anymore either, Jenny.

I'm sorry.

Shooter died off the side of the mountain.

What came back to us last night, it's not Shooter. Not anymore.

I don't know whether to call him Marston or Marswell, but I know he's not from our century, anyway.

This Shooter can still drive a jeep back down Argentine, sure. But he'd be more comfortable astride a horse. Just letting it pick its way.

How I know this, it's the reason I'm here now, talking into your voicemail.

I just popped the lid on what I thought was my crate. It's Shooter's.

His usual stuff for camping, just like mine—we bought a lot of that gear together as well. But tucked into the side is something I know he didn't have coming up the mountain.

It was unfolded on my bed, but I'm trying to fold it back now, before he comes inside, sees.

A full buckskin. Like Marston or Marswell used to drape over the humps he'd sling across the back of his horse, for his trips up into the trees.

I don't know why the buckskin's important to him, Jenny.

I don't care, either.

It's stiff like they can get, but with use it'll soften down.

Don't let it, Jenny.

Don't let him use it.

He's supposed to carry you across a threshold here soon.

It's a bigger threshold than you think, though. It's not one you can come back from. He'll bury you where you'll have a view, and you won't be alone up there either.

And then he'll get interested in the people who might remember the real Shooter. How he used to be. How he isn't anymore.

Jolly Roger. Lex. Kevin Spacey.

I'm not leaving this because of what we used to have, Jenny. I'm leaving this for you because I'm weak, because I'm scared, because I don't want to find Shooter waiting for me in the dark.

You have to listen, Jenny.

I'm the one who let Shooter die. I was the one behind the wheel. I was the one who didn't say anything at the campfire that night.

But I can stop it, too. If you'll listen to me. If you'll . . .

All right, all right, he's not at the truck. Shit. Shit shit shit. I'm going to hang up, I've got to get this back into the crate, just, when you play this, be sure he's not—

∽

STEPHEN GRAHAM JONES

Stephen Graham Jones is the author of sixteen novels, six collections, and two or three hundred stories. His most recent books are the horror novella *Mapping the Interior*, from Tor, and the comic book *My Hero*, from Hex Publishers. Stephen lives in Boulder, Colorado.

THE MADAM IN
ROOM 217

SAM W. ANDERSON

2016

Two years to the day, Jonathan Keller returned to the Hotel De Paris in Georgetown. This time alone and with enough equipment to weigh down the VW bus so it never exceeded forty-five miles-per-hour up the mountain inclines. To be honest though, it probably wouldn't have reached that speed without a cargo. Even more honest, he had no idea how most of the equipment worked.

He limped around the two-story building upon arrival, taking more pictures than he'd need and shooting footage simply to delay going inside. The July sun was merciless. Sweat beaded on his brow, although most of that could be attributed to nerves. Jonathan confirmed the veranda's location, or the lack thereof. He recalled it on the west side, but as the police reports confirmed, no veranda existed. Hadn't since the 1973 renovations according to the hotel manager's testimony, but even he couldn't explain the infamous photo.

Inside, the desk clerk remembered him. She shot Jonathan a look that called him every nasty name at once without uttering a word. "Returning to the scene of the crime, Mr. Keller?"

Jonathan put on his most charming smile, although it didn't work as well anymore. "My room ready?"

Somehow the crusty glare turned crustier. "I don't know why management agreed to this. Make it easier on everybody. Turn around. Crawl back under your rock in Hollywood."

"I gotta say, your attitude isn't doing much for your Yelp review."

"Does this help?" The woman, middle-aged, slightly chunky, bespectacled, and an apparent life-long employee shot out her middle finger and situated it inches from Jonathan's face.

"If I recall, the hotel reached out to us. I didn't ask for anything that followed. Truth be told, I'm the aggrieved party here."

"We didn't ask for what happened, either. Frankly, Mr. Keller, I'd prefer to forget you ever existed."

He smirked smugly and slipped his Master Card across the counter. "I'll be here all week. I'm sure your disposition will improve. I tend to grow on people."

"You start trouble again, you won't be here half a day." The clerk punished the computer keys with each stroke. She checked him in without making eye contact, hatred simmering and seething, and slid the key card across the counter with such force, it spilled over the edge. "Room 217 again. I trust you'll tote your bags yourself."

Jonathan picked the card from the floor, nodded at the woman, and headed for the stairs. He whistled Bernard Herrmann's Twisted Nerve refrain, half to antagonize the clerk, half to calm himself. He paused at the staircase, inhaled and headed up, dragging his gimpy left foot over each step.

He thought he was ready to face what the hell had happened that night. At least, figure out the reasons why it all went down.

～∞～

"You ever get tired of people hating you?" Lorelei set the camera atop its tripod. She peered through the viewer to catch a shirtless Jonathan gyrating in some exaggerated dance before the open second-floor window. His blond hair bounced, and his muscles rippled with every movement. He clutched a Budweiser tall-boy.

"They don't hate me. I'm one loveable SOB. They hate my character."

"Pretty sure it's you. Reality TV means you're the character." She clicked the record button, thinking the goofy dance would make fine footage for the episode's ending credits.

"They tuning in, though?"

"Hell yeah, they are."

"And don't the message boards call me 'Handsome Jack?'"

"Hell yeah, they do. And they're right, too."

"Then let them hate."

Lorelei joined her husband and performed a bastard-ized version of the Watusi.

"Shake it girl." Both clapped for musical accompaniment.

The heat inside the hotel room ratcheted a degree or three from the activity. Jonathan reached for her, rested his hands and beer can on her waist, and they broke into the box step, executing it as poorly as possible. It was a joke they'd shared since their dating days, and somehow it always crumpled them with laughter. When he went to kiss her, Lorelei thought: There goes the credits footage.

But before things got carried away, a knock rapped on the door. "Production meeting," Ernie yelled. "Room 214, five minutes."

"Five minutes." Jonathan raised his eyebrows in a playful gesture. "We could do it twice!"

"We'll be there," Lorelei shouted back as she pushed Jonathan away. She skipped to the door, undid the bolt and pulled on the knob. It didn't budge. "Very funny, Ernie. Let go."

No answer. She checked the peephole. No Ernie. She pulled the door again, but it wouldn't give. "Damn old hotels." More jiggling of the knob. "You going to stand there looking pretty, or you gonna help me?" She jammed her shoulder into it a couple of times, but to no avail. The knob turned slippery as her hands sweat. The room's temperature had increased a few more degrees. "Jonathan?"

When she turned to see what the delay was, she spotted him splayed across the bed. Not asleep, though. His body, glistened with sweat, convulsed with his back arching and veins bulging from his arms and neck. The bed rattled violently against the hardwood floor. The tall-boy spilled out on the mattress.

The camera, tripod and all, crashed to the hardwood. With a whoosh, the window slammed, cracking the pane through its center.

Lorelei reached again for the door, but the knob burned her hand, and the scent of scorched flesh wafted. "Jonathan!" She sprinted for the bed and shook him by the shoulder with her uninjured hand. His eyes had rolled back, and foam dribbled from his mouth. "Baby!" She cocked her arm to slap him.

Before she could deliver the blow, he shot straight up, eyes returning. The bed ceased shaking. The door opened. The temperature dropped a good ten degrees.

"What the hell happened?" Jonathan asked.

Lorelei inspected him, unsure if she should buy what she'd witnessed, she searched for any tell on his face. Her heart thundered with such force she heard it pulse through her head. "You do that?"

Jonathan shook his head. He gulped breaths as if trying to recover from a strenuous run.

"How'd you do that with the door knob?" She displayed her hand and pointed to the small blister forming in her left palm. "We need some footage of this."

Another rap on the door. Ernie leaned inside. "Let's go, Kellers. Time is money, and I ain't got enough of either."

"You're getting really good at this, Baby," she said to Jonathan. "This is going to rock."

                ✺

Despite the clerk's refusal to assist him, Jonathan tracked down a porter who'd delivered his equipment to room 217. Except for the duffle bag of champagne bottles. Jonathan lugged that himself, preferring not to have to answer for them. The sole condition, besides the exorbitant fee, management stipulated was Jonathan couldn't drink this visit. A condition he intended to honor, but still didn't want to explain how the champagne wasn't for him.

Now, on his third day locked in the room 217, the champagne taunted. He'd kept a couple of bottles on ice in case his visitor ever showed herself.

His mind messed with him, as well. Each noise, he assigned some otherworldly explanation, but he didn't know if they originated from Lorelei or Mattie Silks, or maybe Handsome Jack Ready himself. In the end, most simply were the result of his mind going batty with boredom.

"Maybe I just don't remember things properly," he said into the camera. He'd purposely allowed his stubble to sprout and hadn't touched his hair. Thought it made him gritty and the scene more intense. He spoke in hushed tones for dramatic effect. "Maybe I... Maybe it was just the crew messing around and things got out of hand."

He looked over both shoulders, then leaned into the camera. "Confession time: Most of the things you saw on Keller's Paranormal Journal… well… to put it nicely, they were fabricated. We lived by one rule—the 'Any Rule.' Any crew member could set up any stunt at any time and not tell anybody. Maybe the crew rigged everything that night and they've kept mum. Especially after seeing what I went through with the courts and what not." He thought that'd be a good cut to put in some of the news footage from the past two years.

"Lorelei encouraged the crew to scare us. The worse the scare, the better the TV, and she would have killed to make good TV." He tried forcing a tear, but couldn't. Thoughts of Lorelei only brought numbness now, and he'd cried himself out while in jail. "Instead, she died trying to make good TV."

He clicked off the record button and cursed under his breath for being melodramatic, but reasoned he needed to be. With no network backing, his little YouTube channel was his only path for a comeback. He'd blown the rest of Lorelei's life insurance cash on this excursion. No longer able to rely on effects, he needed to make himself the center of everything. Which was fine—he always thought himself the star of the show, anyhow.

Hitting record again, he walked the camcorder to the instruments. "The EMF meter shows nothing. Still. Two days and not a single instrument has registered squat."

He turned the camera to himself. "I'm running out of time to clear myself. At least in the court of public opinion. Something better happen soon, or this will make me look worse." He stopped recording and wondered what he could do next.

Photographs spread across the desk table, arranged in the most striking manner possible. Taking a few seconds on each photo, he zoomed in for a close up on the most pertinent to his "investigation."

"This is Mattie Silks, infamous madam. Funny how beauty standards change over time. This plump harlot was considered one of the most beautiful women of the old west. And, romanticizing aside, a cold-hearted businessperson."

He caught a drop of sweat before it sullied the photos. "This here, is the famous photo from my trial. As you can clearly see, a veranda did indeed exist on the second-floor's west side. No other photo we took showed this, but clearly it's there." Jonathan cleared his throat. "Over ten experts at the trial testified this photo was not doctored, and not one could explain the veranda."

Jonathan stopped before focusing on the most famous photo, though. He'd cross that bridge when he couldn't avoid it any longer, and would dread facing it every second until his week concluded. Setting the camera aside, he sat on the unmade bed.

The room wasn't as hot as he remembered, but sweat still soaked his Ghostbusters t-shirt. The ceiling fan hadn't worked two years ago, and apparently the maintenance staff was as committed as the wench at the front desk. The fan taunted Jonathan as he laid back. He reached into the ice bucket, fished out half-melted cubes from the water and rubbed them over his forehead. Unconsciously, he found his hand back in the bucket, grasping a bottle.

When he realized this, he jolted from the bed. Camera in tow, he strode to the door. It opened easily—to his disappointment.

The hallway was much more comfortable, the air conditioning functioning there. Still, Jonathan's chest tightened every time he entered the corridor. He swallowed a breath, hit record and began what would probably be the most difficult segment of the episode. The window on the west end of the hall came into focus. The new paint didn't quite match the wall surrounding the replaced window. He struggled keeping the frame from shaking. He thought he could write that off to his limp, but his trembling hands accounted for the majority.

"And here's where it all happened."

Ernie handed out the script to the usual unruly, surly comments from the four-person crew. Jonathan and Lorelei entered room 214 to these familiar jeers. Jonathan carried a six pack and bottle of Makers Mark. Lorelei brought a smartass grin and a command of the room.

"Quiet down degenerates. We're here for three days, but if we wrap this in two, the network would be elated." Ernie spoke like somebody ten years older, although Lorelei could never pin down his exact age. He shaved his head, and his dark skin displayed no wrinkles. A beer gut hung over his belt, but his arms were large and firm. His entire wardrobe consisted of Levis and white t-shirts. "Time is money—"

"And you ain't got enough of either," the group answered in unison.

Jonathan dealt the beers and opened the bottle. Lorelei noticed this becoming more of a ritual than she felt comfortable with, but understood the stress of the show incited a lot of the behavior. After the season, she vowed, she'd sit down with her husband for a long talk about all of the mess.

"We're going to focus on Mattie Silks and Handsome Jack Ready." Ernie popped his beer top. "She was a madam in several towns across the old west, and he was a prick."

"Sounds about right," Lorelei said.

"In the 1870's, she operated a brothel across town, but special clients were brought to the Hotel De Paris. Some stories say these clients were never seen again."

"Ohhhhh," Justin, the camera operator, said in his ghostliest voice. Ernie's nephew, he sported an afro straight out of a Pam Grier movie and spent the majority of his waking hours sharing quality time with his good friend, Mr. Cannabis.

"The hotel wants to play up on the haunted thing to bring in more business, so anything goes, got me?" Ernie continued. "As far as they and we are concerned, Mattie Silks still operates in this hotel, specifically in room 217."

Lorelei stood and positioned herself next to Ernie. "If y-all keep up what you've started, we're going to do right by the Hotel De Paris. I'm sure we've got some usable content already." She popped open her beer. "Anybody want to take credit for that door knob? You heat it from the outside?"

SAM W. ANDERSON - THE MADAM IN ROOM 217

The crew looked around to each other. Nobody would take credit. That was the game.

"Let's be a little careful with that stuff." She held her hand to show off the blister. "I don't mind giving a little skin for my art, but this shit hurts."

"Nice!" Ernie said. "That's what we're looking for."

"Got it. Burn Lorelei," Travis said in his nerdy-chic way. His title was co-producer, but it meant he did everything nobody else wanted to do.

"All right. Should be dark in three hours. Get whatever interviews you need while Trav hooks up the room."

"Finishes hooking up the room," Lorelei added.

"I ain't been in there, Mrs. Keller. I'd take credit for it, but I can't."

Ernie polished off his beer in a single, long chugging drink. "Nine p.m. Room 217. Be there, on time, so we can meet our deadline."

Jonathan stood, put his hand out, and called the crew to bring it in. "Keller Paranormal Journal on three," he said. "One, two…"

"Fuck you," the crew called as a choir.

◦◦◦

Jonathan must have passed out after the second bottle of champagne. Coming to, his tongue occupied his entire mouth and had grown a fur coat that tasted of sour ass. He reached into the ice bucket and scooped out a couple handfuls of water, the cold liquid the perfect antidote for his parched palette.

163

Sweat glued him to the mattress. His vision took far too long to focus, but when it did, he still couldn't identify what appeared out of place. When he finally figured it out, it wasn't so much the visual as the sound that gave it away. A rhythmic ticking. Dare he hope, a haunting ticking?

From his prone position, he noticed the ceiling fan blades whirling, propelling hot air throughout the narrow room. His stomach lurched when he bolted from the bed. The EMF meter, which read electromagnetic activity, went ballistic.

"Come out, you bitch." He searched the room for the camera. "That you, Mattie? Happy to see me again?"

The fan twirled faster. Jonathan was so caught up in the activity, it didn't occur to him he had zero idea how to communicate with an actual ghost. He fought back the dry heaves and dizziness and hit record.

The camcorder engaged. He zoomed in on the fan. "Day three. Mattie Silks makes an appearance." Adrenaline rushed, forcing alcohol through his veins faster. He directed the shot at the EMF meter. "Clearly, I am not alone. Come out, Mattie. Come out and play."

Despite the confidence he tried projecting, he felt officially freaked. Lorelei had always been the planner of the two. As usual, Jonathan flew by the seat of his shorts, and properly (metaphorically) soiled shorts at that.

His taunts garnered no response, though. He whistled the "Twisted Nerve" melody again until he grew bored. The meter danced, the fan whirled, but other than the room warming, nothing else. For hours. Jonathan chilled another champagne bottle, champagne allegedly being Mattie Silks drink of choice, in the melted ice. Waited for a sign. Listened to the annoying ticking of the chains hanging from the unbalanced ceiling fan. The pattern of the clicks should have been rhythmic, he thought, but they sounded in bursts.

About the time he thought of opening the bottle, thinking a bit of the hair of the dog might calm his queasiness, it finally hit him.

The sounds registered in no pattern after all. They were Morse Code.

Around midnight, to escape the heat of room 217 and a disappointing night of failures, Lorelei and Jonathan snuck to the window located at the west end of the hall and shared a cigarette.

"You think Travis is toking with Justin or something?" Lorelei asked. "It's not like him to fuck up this bad."

"Maybe he shot his wad with that doorknob trick."

"But the whole crew?" She accepted the Virginia Slim from him. "We better figure out something quick. I don't care how good these guys are at editing, we're in some trouble here."

"We got two more days."

"Bullshit. When Ernie says the network prefers two days, we have a day and a half." Lorelei's stomach tumbled onto itself. She hadn't shared the latest ratings. This would be their last season unless the finale pulled off something spectacular, but saw no purpose in stressing Jonathan.

"Hey! There's no smoking in here." The desk clerk stomped up the garish corridor carpet that looked like Timothy Leary had vomited an LSD dream all over it. She slowed as she neared, though. "Oh. Mr. and Mrs. Keller. I didn't realize-"

"We're sorry." Jonathan dialed up smile number ten and Lorelei knew they could have been smoking crack with naked eight-year olds, Jonathan was going to charm their way out. "It's just the altitude. We were worried about making it back up them steps again, ma'am. Can you forgive us this one time? Perhaps you'd join us?"

The woman actually blushed. Lorelei thought she smelled the clerk lubricating her granny panties. Handsome Jack at work.

"I don't smoke. If you two could just open the window, I'll let it slide this time. But if any guests object, I'll have to ask you to stop. Fair?"

"More than, ma'am. You folks are right friendly around here. We appreciate you putting up with our silliness."

"Nonsense, Jack. It's an honor to have you."

"Thank you." Jonathan turned his smile to eleven. "We'll mosey off to bed after finishing up this nasty thing. Sorry we had to bother you."

The woman pivoted and waddled down the hall, an extra giddy-up in her step.

"I think she wants you, Handsome Jack."

"Well, she's only flesh and blood."

"Us poor mortals." Lorelei opened the window further. "How about we finish this outside?"

"What?"

"There's a walkway out there."

"Since when?"

Lorelei wrapped the thin blanket around her. "Dunno. Since Mattie Silks pimped out bitches to silver miners under the nose of her husband, Handsome Jack? Let's get some fresh air." She stepped through the window and onto the veranda. "Your girlfriend, the desk clerk, won't bother us out here."

"I'll be damned." Jonathan grabbed his mostly empty bottle of Makers Mark and joined his wife.

She immediately regretted it. Once Jonathan joined her, the veranda didn't feel as substantial. Somehow, the blanket about her seemed suffocating, and she swore the temperature soared.

Jonathan took no notice though. He pounded the rest of the bottle, then grinned like the Cheshire Cat on pain killers. No way he could have seen the orb over his shoulder.

Reaching for her camera, excitement overwhelmed her, and Lorelei failed in forming a full sentence.

"What is it, babe?"

The orb expanded, drew close enough to her husband, it blurred his face.

"It's Mattie Silks." Lorelei noted Jonathan's laughter moments before the window slammed shut. It trapped the straggling blanket. The orb flashed in a blinding burst, then fled. The veranda collapsed. Disappeared. Lorelei understood her fate before her neck snapped.

Jonathan typed out the coded messages on his laptop. It'd been a few years since Boy Scouts, so he wasn't sure he transcribed everything perfectly, but he got the gist.

"She's with me, Jack."

"You can see her."

"Can you forgive me? I got confused about Handsome Jack."

"She's a good worker. A good earner."

"She misses you."

"She's mad you left her to be a whore."

Jonathan positioned the camera behind him and the laptop's Skype camera was also recording. He didn't know what point he should cut them off, but thought one of them would finally catch him sobbing: The money shot.

"You can be with her."

"For a price. Whores need to be paid, Handsome Jack. Only sluts work for free."

The room had to be over a hundred degrees. Jonathan sweat out the three bottles of champagne and then some. He pounded out Morse Code on the table. "Why? Why her."

"It wasn't her. It was you."

He knocked more, as best his drunken mind could recall. "Let me see her."

"What do you have to offer, Jack?"

He bit back the vomit gorging in his throat. "What would it take?" he asked in a series of dots and dashes.

The fan slowed. Stopped for a moment.

"No!" Jonathan screamed. "Let me see her."

With a new energy, the fan recommenced its swirling. Ferociously, as if it might break free from the ceiling and fly away of its own volition.

"I want to feel flesh again."

"I want to be alive."

"I need a vessel."

Jonathan rapped on the table, each knock sounding wet from the blood bursting via his knuckles. "What vessel? What's a vessel?"

"Give me your body, and your soul can be with her."

"Jonathan." Lorelei's voice. Faint, but unmistakable. It emanated from the Shack Hack – a radio the show had used dozens of times to mimic a ghost's voice. *"Don't leave me here, baby. I can't do this."*

He no longer needed to pretend to cry. "Lor? That you?"

"A body. I need a body if you want to be with her."

"You prepared for this, Handsome Jack?"

"Help me, Jonathan. It's awful."

Jonathan knocked in code again: "A body? Any body?"

"Any body."

"Jonathan, I miss you."

He stood from the desk and paced the room. Sweat fell off him in sheets and champagne clouded his brain.

"She was pregnant, Jack. You know that?"

Jonathan went to the duffle bag and popped open a warm bottle. The alcohol rushed through the opening, spilled onto the floor, and he put his mouth over the gusher, letting it all in.

"Give me a minute," he knocked. After walking over to the phone, he dialed the front desk.

"You ready to leave, Mr. Keller?" the bitchy voice asked.

"Yes. Please help me with my bags."

"I'll send somebody."

"I'd prefer you. I owe you an apology."

A moment of silence. "Fine. I'll be there momentarily."

He hung up. He wrapped on the desk. "I got you a body. I want my wife."

SAM W. ANDERSON

Sam W. Anderson lives in Denver, Colorado with his wife, two kids and the most expensive rescue mutt in history. He's the author of over forty published short stories and collaborative novels, and two short-story collections: *Postcards from Purgatory*, and *American Gomorrah: The Money Run Omnibus*. The latter will be updated and reissued from Rothco Press. *The Nines* is his first solo novel. He likes pie.

HER FIRST HUSBAND

MARIO ACEVEDO

2017

"It was a ghost," Mrs. Felicity Chesterfield said.

I looked at her.

"A ghost," she repeated.

"You've said that." I kept my voice low and reassuring as I glanced at my police laptop. "I read the file." The original investigator working this case had retired, and so dealing with this old lady and her bat-shit crazy ghost story had fallen to me.

We were in a coffee shop on 6th Street in Georgetown, where Felicity insisted on meeting. The weather was especially pleasant, warm and bright, and yet she remained bundled in an oversized sweater, baggy pants, and a gauzy scarf that draped her head chador-style. Her wide-brimmed hat and goggle-like sunglasses reminded me of a Hollywood has-been hiding from time, like the character Gloria Swanson played in *Sunset Boulevard*.

"But it's not the ghost that prompted this meeting," I said. "It's that Annabelle Crosby's son alerted us that eight thousand dollars had been transferred from her bank account into yours."

Felicity didn't answer. I could tell by the angle of her face she wasn't looking at me.

I pressed the obvious. "It looks suspicious."

I didn't have to be Sherlock Holmes to connect the dots. Felicity Chesterfield and Annabelle Crosby had only known each other briefly, and then Crosby went missing, which was almost twenty-four months ago, and her last known whereabouts were Felicity's house. Crosby's son petitioned the court to have her declared dead at the two-year mark so he could claim her estate. A week short of that date, her bank account was suddenly emptied. This caused us to reopen the cold case file that we had on Crosby and look again at Mrs. Felicity Chesterfield as our prime suspect.

I said, "Crosby's account had been accessed from a computer in your house."

"Sandra—" she began.

"Detective Gonzales," I corrected to emphasize that I was on official business.

"Detective Gonzales," she amended. Her voice had a delicate rasp. "I've cooperated with the investigation from the beginning. I allowed the police to search my home. They brought the smeller hounds—"

"Cadaver dogs."

"Yes, them, and they found nothing." She fixed her sunglasses on my face. "My house was turned upside down. The investigators ransacked my kitchen and even took dishes and spices they tested for poison."

And the labs came up with zilch, and I nodded to concede the point.

"They even sprayed that blood detector stuff—"

"Luminol."

"And found nothing," she replied, irritated. The skin on the back of her hands looked thin and papery. She pulled her sweater sleeves to cover her hands to the knuckles. "Like I told the investigators from the beginning, it was the ghost that took Annabelle."

"The same ghost you mentioned during the original investigation?"

"Yes."

"The same ghost whose existence you later recanted?"

"Only to keep from being put on an involuntary mental health hold."

"And now you've changed your mind…again."

Her face tensed. She sat straighter and readjusted her scarf. "It was the ghost. You want to solve this case, you can ask him."

Georgetown is lousy with ghost stories. You can't visit a tea room or traipse into an antique shop without getting your ear bent about the resident spook. The difference was Felicity's ghost was part of a homicide investigation.

"So that I'm not misunderstanding what you're saying, this ghost can tell me what happened to Annabelle Crosby?"

"More than that, he can even show you."

"Where?"

"At my house. Come by at six this evening."

"Why not now?"

"Because I have to summon the ghost first. Otherwise there's no point in coming." Mrs. Chesterfield levered her bony frame from the chair. "You have my address. See you then."

❧

Twilight comes early to Georgetown. It's nestled right up against the mountains directly to the west. When the sun drops behind the ridge, it's as if a door closes, it gets dark that fast.

Felicity's home was set back into the slope and to get there meant driving along Main Street, itself a misnomer because it's just a dirt road that runs parallel to and right along the mountain. Her place was at the end of a short looping drive that split from the road.

As I turned the corner and her house came into view. The glow from her windows beckoned. I pulled to a stop beside her front porch. When I realized I stopped right over the same spot where Crosby's car had been abandoned, a tingle of apprehension plucked my nerves. I'm not superstitious but I've worn a badge long enough to listen to these hunches. So I backed up and parked about fifty feet over.

I checked my cell phone. Six o'clock. There wasn't much to Felicity's house—a narrow, clapboard house, painted canary yellow, white trim, the colors grayed by the gathering dusk. Lacey white curtains at the two windows at the front of the house, one in the door and

174

the other in the wall, obscured the interior from prying eyes. A typical Georgetown bungalow built around the 1920s. Dead plants stuck out of clay pots set on the porch. The back of the house had been carved into the rocky slope, and the tangled branches of pines and aspens leaned over it like a shroud.

Felicity lived by herself. She had been born in 1942 according to one record, 1936 in another, and a hit on a genealogy search listed her as Felicity Olstad (her maiden name) and born April 9, 1898. Whatever her actual age, she was old, and if I had a problem handling her, then I should hand in my badge and gun.

I sensed Felicity wanted to come clean about what happened to Crosby. After all, when she transferred money from Crosby's account, she had to have known someone would notice. Or maybe not. Criminals have done stupider things for much less than 8,000 dollars. If I waited, then I could lose this chance to close this case. Like real estate, getting a break in a crime investigation can be all about timing.

Once out of my car, I clipped my badge and ID to the front of my jacket and tapped my pistol where it was holstered to my waist. I couldn't see any situation where I'd have to shoot a frail thing like Felicity, but something bad had happened to Crosby, and I wanted to be ready for anything.

I strode onto the porch and pressed the doorbell. Footsteps shuffled to the door. A silhouette darkened the curtain, it parted, but I couldn't see who was looking out. The deadbolt snapped, and the door swung inward.

Felicity beamed. Her brown eyes were shockingly bright, like a lamp shining through amber. "Detective Gonzales." She still wore her outfit from earlier, minus the hat, scarf, and sunglasses. Her white hair fell loose to her shoulders. "Please come in." She stepped back and when I passed, she looked out the door. "Are you alone?"

"I am," I replied, then added, "the department knows I'm here," and felt sheepish for saying this.

My senses were on full alert, primed to detect anything out of the ordinary. I sniffed a perfumy fragrance, like from a scented candle. I compared the layout of the house to that described in the case file. We were in the front room, which resembled a Victorian parlor—a velvet sofa and matching armchair, dark wood furnishings, crystal bric-a-brac everywhere, a Persian rug. A lot of elderly shut-ins tended to be hoarders, so I was surprised how neat and orderly the place was. Even so, the interior seemed claustrophobic instead of cozy.

She closed and locked the door. "The ghost is waiting."

Her mentioning the ghost made my mouth go dry as dust. *Get a grip*, I scolded myself. The only ghosts I've seen were in the movies, and in those circumstances when a crime was involved, the "ghost" was actually a picture or video projected on smoke, or a veil, or some other contrived bullshit the main characters were too stupid to notice. I scoped out the ceiling and saw nothing but the electric light fixtures.

"Once I meet this ghost," I worked to keep the sarcasm out of my voice, "he'll tell me everything?"

"Not tell exactly, but you'll see."

Felicity led me from the parlor to a second room, occupied by a small dining table with two chairs. Heavy velvet curtains were drawn tight over the window. At the far corner of the room stood an oval floor mirror, the glass covered by a black cloth.

Lit candles stood on the table and on the narrow shelf to my right. Their flames knit threads of smoke that were the source of that spicy, floral scent. The room darkened, and the candle flames seemed to flare brighter. My legs hitched a step and my breath caught. Felicity was by the mirror, and I didn't see how she dimmed the lights. I was beginning to feel off center, and the cloying smell from the candles was getting sickly sweet.

"Welcome, Detective Sandra Gonzales," a voice from behind me said.

Nerves zinging to maximum red alert, I spun around, heart racing, right hand on my pistol.

A man stood behind me, maybe five feet away. He was dressed like he'd stepped here from the 19th century—a loose frock coat, vest over a collar-less shirt, baggy pants. He was about my height, five-nine, but paunchy, maybe 180 pounds. Sad, dark eyes peered from a round face. A thin mustache drooped from under his round, knob-like nose.

But I could see right through him.

The ghost.

I blinked, thinking I had to be hallucinating, but every time my eyes opened the ghost was still here. I didn't want to believe what I was seeing. My gaze stabbed all around him, trying to spot some kind of a projector.

But there wasn't any. The floral candle smell was now an odor that made my head feel heavy.

Felicity put her hand on my shoulder as if to keep me steady. "Meet my first husband, Eliphalet Chesterfield. He proved to be such a bore that I got so sick of him and I…Eliphalet, show the detective."

The ghost unfastened the top button of his shirt and pulled it down as he tilted his head back. His throat split wide like a second mouth.

My thoughts recoiled in horror. Eighteen years I've been a cop, faced countless lowlifes, gotten in plenty of fights and high-speed pursuits, been shot at, have my heart pumping so hard I'd thought it was going to explode right out of my chest, but I have never experienced the dread that enveloped me now. I should've reacted, drawn my gun, but my mind panicked, screaming for my body to do something but my arms and legs remained frozen.

"He's got plenty of other gashes in his back, but that's the one that did him in. I buried him in the crawl space of our home. Given how investigations were conducted back then, no one doubted my word that he'd run off and left me."

The ghost smoothed his neck and refastened his collar.

"But Eliphalet, stubborn like everyone else in his mule-headed family, refused to die. His ghost returned to haunt me, not to get even but because he missed me, the poor softhearted fool. Though I've been widowed many times since I filleted Eliphalet, I was fond of the name Chesterfield and have kept it since."

Eliphalet gazed at me, the candle smoke drifting through his translucent form.

I had to be dreaming. This was a nightmare. Inside, my heart and guts boiled with terror, but when I tried to move, nothing. All I could do was blink. And smell. That odor worked itself through my nose and down my throat. It seeped through my flesh. Then a new thought ripped the bottom of my fears and I found myself dropping into an abyss of horror.

I was like a spider's prey that had been bitten. The poison worked through me, not killing me, but keeping me alive and paralyzed. When Felicity took the 8,000 dollars from Crosby's account, it had been bait, and I was the one who was trapped in her web.

She grabbed my shoulders and slowly rotated me to face the mirror. "Which brings us to why you're here, Detective Gonzales. Eliphalet showed me how to cheat death, and specifically Father Time. A girl must do what she can to look young. Yes, detective, I was born 1898. I am that old."

She whisked off the cloth and inside the mirror, her hands pressed against the inside of the glass, stood Annabelle Crosby, still wearing the clothes she had worn when she went missing. She was 42 at the time but now looked ancient and wilted, like she'd been drained of life, more desiccated corpse than human being. Her dry eyes latched onto me as she mouthed a muffled scream. "Get out! Get out!"

My inner voice roared, shaking my nerves. *Save yourself! Do what you must. Run. Kill.* But I remained motionless. My mind pounded futilely against the switches in my brain, ordering my arms and legs into action.

But nothing.

Felicity said, "Feeding on a man doesn't work, which is unfortunate because they're much easier to catch. So sister nourishes sister." She reached through the glass and grabbed Annabelle by the face. Her fingers sank into Annabelle's flesh like meat hooks clawing through hamburger. Annabelle squirmed and batted her hands. Felicity set her jaw and yanked her arm back. Annabelle's body whooshed out of her clothes. Still pulling her by the face, Felicity backed away from the mirror and dragged Annabelle's naked, withered carcass until she lay prone across the floor like an empty sack.

I could hear myself wailing, the shrieks of terror echoing in my skull. I wanted to wet myself but my body was no longer mine. I could only swivel my eyes to watch Felicity.

She grabbed one of Crosby's arms and planted one foot against the small of her back. She twisted the arm in one direction and then the other, the flesh around Annabelle's shoulder tearing loose with a wet, gooey rip. She offered the arm to Eliphalet who snatched it greedily and munched like he was gulping down a hoagie. Felicity tore off the other arm and chomped into it.

I was overcome with nausea, and the spectacle was so surreal, so horrifying, that to keep from blacking out, my mind seemed to float disconnected from this macabre scene.

Felicity kept tearing the body to pieces, which she and Eliphalet crunched and devoured like hungry dogs. As she swallowed the last piece of Crosby, her face filled out, the wrinkles erasing, her hair becoming a rich golden color, and her stooped frame straightened and gained an athletic tone. "Not as satisfying as feeding on her soul," she smacked her lips, "but waste not, want not." She nodded at the ghost.

Eliphalet advanced toward me, arms raised.

My heart pounding, tears burning my eyes, I tried to shrink from him, but I remained rooted in place, helpless.

When his hands touched my shoulders, his fingers were iron-hard and ice cold. He nudged me against the mirror. I tipped backwards and was immersed in the sensation of plunging through a film of water. I toppled against a rough floor and lay there for a moment. In reflex, I reached for my face…

…and incredibly my hand came up. The paralysis was gone! I scrambled to my feet only to realize that I was in a tiny room, illuminated solely by the light of an oval-shaped window. I was looking out through the mirror. I lunged at the glass and I might as well have thrown myself against a wall of steel.

Screaming, I beat my fists against the inside of the mirror.

Felicity brought her face to the glass. She was dabbing makeup on her cheeks. "Get comfortable, you'll be there a while. It depends on when I get my next victim." She started winding a scarf around her head. "For now, I have to prepare myself for when your compatriots come asking about you. And just where did you disappear to, Detective Gonzales?"

She arranged the black cloth over the mirror, and the room went dark.

❧

MARIO ACEVEDO

Mario Acevedo is the author of the bestselling Felix Gomez detective-vampire series, which includes *Rescue From Planet Pleasure* from WordFire Press. His forthcoming book is a middle-grade science-fiction novel, *University of Doom* (Hex Publishers). He edited the Colorado Book Award Finalist anthology *Found* for the Rocky Mountain Fiction Writers (RMFW Press) and contributed stories to award-winning anthologies *Nightmares Unhinged* and *Cyber World* (Hex Publishers). Mario lives and writes in Denver, Colorado.

ME, MY SELF, AND TOM

AFTERWORD

BRIAN KEENE

MAY 2017

Tom Piccirilli wasn't so much a writer as he was a magician with words. During his career, he wrote nearly fifty books and over two hundred short stories, and jumped genres the way you or I change underwear. The spines of his novels, novellas, and collections were emblazoned with every genre category you can name—Mystery, Horror, Thriller, Crime, Noir, Western, Bizarro, Science-Fiction, Non-Fiction, Fantasy, Erotica, Comic Books, Poetry, and so much more. Like his fiction, he amassed awards across the various genre platforms, as well—two International Thriller Writers Awards, five Bram Stoker Awards, and a finalist for both the Edgar Allan Poe Award and the Fantasy Award, among others.

Tom was a writer's writer, meaning he was an author other authors showered with acclaim and accolades—a writer the rest of us held up as the best of us, the one we always mentioned when fans asked us, "Who are we reading?" He made his home with both commercial mainstream publishers and the small press, and while Hollywood success and pop culture notoriety might have escaped him (except for the 1995 direct-to-video *Addicted to Murder*, a *Hellboy* media tie-in, and an issue of *The Punisher* for Marvel Comics), he was worshipped and adored by those who use words for a living, and by those readers for whom words are like manna, as essential to their well-being as water and oxygen. His fans included Ken Bruen, Stephen King, Dean Koontz, Ed Gorman, T.M. Wright, Joe R. Lansdale, Richard Laymon, Greg Rucka, Keith Giffen, and countless other masters of the written word—all of whom are stylistically different, but all of whom dug the uniqueness of Tom's prose.

Regardless of which genre he was writing in, his prose always had a poetic, lyrical quality to it. He had a way of grabbing—nay, commanding—your attention from the very start. Take these opening sentences, as way of example. "We move in spasms" is the opening sentence to his novel *A Choir of Ill Children*, describing three conjoined triplets. When we first meet Terry Rand, the anti-hero protagonist of *The Last Kind Words*, he tells us "I'd come five years and two thousand miles to stand in the rain while they prepared my brother for his own murder." Tom did things with words that made you laugh: "Gray invited me up to the insane asylum hootenanny" (from *Frayed*). Tom did things with words that made you hurt: "Coincidence only carries so far, and then you've just got to figure the universe wants to fuck you up as much as possible" (from *Fuckin' Lie Down Already*). Tom did things with words that filled you with dread: "Despite the fiery omen of murder burning over their table, the couple seemed perfectly content" (from *A Lower Deep*). Tom did things with words that made you wonder: "Flynn remembered the night of his death more clearly than any other in his life" (from *The Midnight Road*). Opening sentences, all of them, wielded as deftly and decisively as a barbarian with a sword, or a sniper with a rifle.

Or a sorcerer with a spell.

I was always in awe of Tom's ability to weave that magic. Perhaps that is why his "Self" series of short stories—about a nameless Necromancer and his demonic familiar—have always been among my favorites of his work. Indeed, I named one of my cats (now deceased) after Self. "Neverdead", the first of the Self tales, appeared in *Terminal Fright* #6 in 1994. Roughly a dozen more stories and a full-length novel (*A Lower Deep*) followed. Most of the stories were collected in the now out-of-print *Deep Into That Darkness Peering*. Ostensibly, Tom's Necromancer character was just another addition to the long-line of fictional occult detectives. That lineage includes Sheridan Le Fanu's Dr. Martin Hesselius, Bram Stoker's Dr. Abraham Van Helsing, Algernon Blackwood's John Silence, William Hope Hodgson's Carnacki the Ghost Finder, Manly Wade Wellman's Silver John and John Thunstone, Robert E. Howard's Steve Harrison, F. Paul Wilson's Repairman Jack, Laurell K Hamilton's Anita Blake, Jonathan Maberry's Sam Hunter, DC Comics characters John Constantine and The Phantom Stranger, and my own Levi Stoltzfus. But, like he did with all his prose, Tom's Self stories transcended the trappings of that particular genre niche. The Necromancer's journey—his story arc—is a quest for answers. What answers? The same answers we all seek. Black or white, Christian or Muslim, Conservative or Progressive—we all want to know why we are here, and what happens after this. The Necromancer is a fictional character, but like so many of Tom's characters, he is instilled with life, with humanity. He is us. He is Tom.

Tom and I had many discussions over the years about bleeding onto the page—a term we both favored in describing our method of mining our real-life experiences, particularly our hurts and heartaches and fears, and using them to imbue our fiction. Tom once said in an interview, "Some writers bleed onto the page. I suspect others, like Brian and myself, hemorrhage."

Tom had a lot of recurring themes that appeared in his prose and poetry, regardless of which genre he was writing. Having lost his father, Edward William Piccirilli, at an early age, fatherhood and parenting and the particular relationship between fathers and sons informs much of what he wrote in blood. So do loss, mourning, and mutation. When he met his soulmate, Michelle, love became a recurring theme, as well, perhaps written from the blood of his heart.

Brotherhood was another theme. Personally, I always liked it best when Tom wrote about brothers. He was one of my best friends for nearly twenty years. We always called each other "Big Bro" and "Little Bro" because that's what we were. When he and Michelle got married, he introduced me as such to his family members at the reception: "This is Brian. He's our little brother!"

I met Tom in the mid-Nineties, when the Internet was still in its infancy, and the horror genre was going through a dry spell. Although he was only two years older than me, he had already experienced some early success, with the publication of two novels, several novellas, dozens of short stories and poems, and a few editing gigs. We used to both hang out in a chat room with other horror writers. Most of the users were novices, but Richard Laymon, Ray Garton, and Tom were there, freely dispensing advice and encouragement. Laymon and Garton's advice always had the benefit of years—the sage wisdom of authors who had already seen and done it all, and could look back with clarity. Tom's advice was more immediate. Despite his early success, he was right there in the trenches with us, fighting for sales to the same publications, but always cheering us on and offering guidance from his unique perspective. Sometimes, he let his own work slide in order to help us with ours. He warned us about the many snakes and charlatans who inhabit this field. He watched out for us, just like any big brother would.

But his tutelage went beyond professional. Growing up, I was always jealous of friends whose big brothers turned them on to music or comics or movies that none of us younger kids had been exposed to yet. Tom provided me my first exposure to the films of Alejandro Jodorowsky and John Woo, the writings of Raymond

Chandler and Lucius Shepard, and the fever dream that is *Riki-Oh: The Story of Riki*. For years, we regularly sent each other care packages of comic books and movies and old paperbacks. Every time one of those boxes showed up in the mail, it was like every major holiday and a birthday all rolled into one.

There won't be any more of those packages. But he's left behind an incredible body of work, and a ton of memorable advice on the craft. My favorite was always this: "If your response to being stranded alone on a desert island is to scratch stories in the sand with a stick, then you're a writer."

Tom Piccirilli was a writer's writer. But he was also a brother to a lot of those writers, as well. Not just to me. His professional family was large, spanning across those multiple genres he wrote in. He traveled from genre to genre, borne by the whims of his always active muse, and the professionals who inhabited those various genres— professionals who never seem to agree on anything—all agreed that they loved Tom.

I miss him. As I said, there will be no more of those care packages. No more visiting him and Michelle in Colorado, or lounging at conventions, smoking cigars and drinking good bourbon talking about books and women and movies and life. No more crazy road trips together. I'm left with all the books and movies he sent over the years, and the set of pasta bowls he and Michelle once bought me as a present, and a thousand good memories that make me smile.

And you are left with that eclectic, beautiful body of work.

Read it. This was his blood, which was shed for you.

If you read it, then Tom, much like the Necromancer and his sidekick Self, will continue to transcend death.

Which is a pretty neat trick—one that is unachievable for most of humankind.

But not for Tom.

I told you. The guy was a magician.

Brian Keene
Somewhere along the Susquehanna River
May 2017

༄

BRIAN KEENE

Brian Keene writes novels, comic books, short fiction, and occasional journalism for money. He is the author of over forty books, mostly in the horror, crime, and dark fantasy genres. His 2003 novel, *The Rising*, is often credited (along with Robert Kirkman's *The Walking Dead* comic and Danny Boyle's *28 Days Later* film) with inspiring pop culture's current interest in zombies. In addition to his own original work, Keene has written for media properties such as *Doctor Who, The X-Files, Hellboy, Masters of the Universe*, and *Alien*. Several of Keene's novels have been developed for film, including *Ghoul, The Naughty List, The Ties That Bind*, and *Fast Zombies Suck*. Several more are in-development or under option. Keene also serves as Executive Producer for the independent film studio Drunken Tentacle Productions.

The father of two sons, Keene lives in rural Pennsylvania.

ABOUT THE EDITORS

Jeanne C. Stein is the national bestselling author of the Urban Fantasy series, The Anna Strong Vampire Chronicles and most recently, The Fallen Siren Series written as S. J. Harper. She is active in the writing community, belonging to Rocky Mountain Fiction Writers, Sisters in Crime and Horror Writers of America. There are nine books in the Anna Strong series and two books and two novellas in a new series written with Samantha Sommersby under the S. J. Harper pseudonym. She also has more than a dozen short story credits, including the novella, *Blood Debt*, from the New York Times bestselling anthology, *Hexed* (2011) and The NYT bestselling anthology, *Dead But Not Forgotten* edited by Charlaine Harris (2014.) Her short stories have been published in collections here in the US and the UK. Her latest, an Anna Strong novella entitled *Anna and the Vampire Prince*, was recently published by Hex Publishers.

Joshua Viola is an author, artist, and former video game developer (*Pirates of the Caribbean, Smurfs, TARGET: Terror*). In addition to creating a transmedia franchise around *The Bane of Yoto*, honored with more than a dozen awards, he is the author of *Blackstar*, a tie-in novel based on the discography of Celldweller. His debut horror anthology, *Nightmares Unhinged*, was a *Denver Post* and Amazon bestseller, and named one of the Best Books of 2016 by Kirkus Reviews. His second anthology, *Cyber World* (co-edited by Jason Heller), was a Colorado Book Award Finalist and named one of the Best Books of 2016 by Barnes & Noble. His short fiction has appeared in The Rocky Mountain Fiction Writers' *Found* anthology (RMFW Press), *D.O.A. III – Extreme Horror Collection* (Blood Bound Books), and *The Literary Hatchet* (PearTree Press). He lives in Denver, Colorado, where he is chief editor and owner of Hex Publishers.

CPSIA information can be obtained
at www.ICGtesting.com
Printed in the USA
FSOW04n1055150617
35223FS

9 780998 666754